Panchlight and Other Stories

Phanishwar Nath Renu (1921–77) was born in the village of Aurahi Hingna in the Purnea district of Bihar. His novel *Maila Anchal* (1954) hailed him as a stalwart in the *Nayi Kahani* (New Story) movement. His short story *Maare Gaye Gulfam* was made into a major Hindi feature film. Renu's work speaks to the reader of all that is enduring in the human heart.

Rakhshanda Jalil has edited two collections of short stories and published six works of translations. Her recent books include *Invisible City: The Hidden Monuments of Delhi* (Niyogi, 2008) and *Naked Voices and other Stories*, a translation of stories and sketches by Manto (Roli/Permanent Black, 2008). She works as Director, Media and Culture at Jamia Millia Islamia, New Delhi.

Panchlight and Other Stories

Phanishwar Nath Renu

Translated from the Hindi and with an Introduction by

Rakhshanda Jalil

Orient BlackSwan

ORIENT BLACKSWAN PRIVATE LIMITED

Registered Office
3-6-752 Himayatnagar, Hyderabad 500 029 (A.P.), India
e-mail: centraloffice@orientblackswan.com

Other Offices
Bangalore, Bhopal, Bhubaneshwar, Chennai,
Ernakulam, Guwahati, Hyderabad, Jaipur, Kolkata,
Lucknow, Mumbai, New Delhi, Patna

First published 2010

ISBN: 978-81-250-3841-2

Typeset in Adobe Garamond 11/14.2 by
InoSoft Systems, Noida

Printed in India at
De Unique, New Delhi

Published by
Orient Blackswan Private Limited
1/24 Asaf Ali Road, New Delhi 110 002
e-mail: delhi@orientblackswan.com

Contents

Translator's Introduction

Phanishwar Nath Renu (1921–77), born in a modest farmer's home in village Aurahi Hingna—then in Purnea district of Bihar, but now part of Araria district—is regarded as one of the foremost Hindi writers of his time. Renu, as he was popularly known, is the only Hindi writer, after Premchand, who reached across to a national audience—one that was larger and more pluralistic than his core readership within the Hindi-speaking 'cow-belt'. Like Premchand, he too wrote of class, caste and gender prejudices in rural, often marginalised and disenfranchised societies. But, there are no stock characters in Renu's stories, no rhetorical exaggerations and, certainly, none of the hyperbolic speeches and sermonising on social evils that seem jarring to the modern reader. Instead, there is a far more sophisticated social commentary, speech that is completely natural and grounded in the local dialect, and a ruthlessly realistic portrayal of society and of his characters. What is more, there are large dollops of wit, humour and satire, along with oodles of folksongs and snatches of poetry thrown in for good measure!

Dogged by ill-health and ill-luck, Renu never quite reached the heights that contemporaries such as Agyeya, Yashpal and Jainendra did. Maybe because he chose causes that were close to his heart but politically ill-advised, such as the underground freedom struggle in Nepal and the till-then-fledgling Naxalite movements in various tribal pockets in the Mayurbhanj area of Orissa. Regardless of our sympathy, or the lack of it, for the ideology that drove him, it is difficult to ignore the compelling honesty in his writing. It is equally difficult to miss the sheer humaneness that pervades Renu's worldview and permeates every single one of his characters, making them seem like 'one of us' even though they are located in a milieu very far removed from anything we might have ever known. Because of the amazing ability to look deep into the human heart and the human predicament, Renu's writing rises above the small and the immediate. He writes of passions spent, hurts unresolved and dreams unfulfilled, in the context of a rapidly changing social fabric and a crumbling social order.

With *Maila Aanchal*, published in 1954, Renu became a force to be reckoned with in the *Nayi Kahani* (New Story) movement. This reputation was shored up with a slew of short stories published during the 1950s and 1960s, most notably *Maare Gaye Gulfam,* which was picturised as *Teesri Kasam* with Raj Kapoor and Waheeda Rehman in lead roles, and Iftekhar and Asit Sen in finely-etched, memorable cameos. Directed by Basu Bhattacharya and produced by the film lyricist, Shailendra, in 1966, it catapulted Renu to national fame. It showed how a love story set in rural Bihar—of Hiraman, a bullock-cart driver, and Hirabai, a dancer in a traveling dance company—could capture the national imagination. It also helped underscore the point that in branding Renu as the pioneer of the *aanchalik upanyas* (regional novel), the literary critics were not only doing Renu a grave disservice by virtually painting him into a box, but were also guilty of circulating an oxymoron, a contradiction in terms. While, admittedly, based in rural Bihar, Renu's stories were not parochial. Far from it, in fact!

Having read an odd story here or there, what drew me to Renu and led me to explore his vast oeuvre was precisely this quality of universality that seemed so alluring. The ability to transcend the here-and-now and speak of universal concerns—always the hallmark of a great writer—seems especially unusual, coming as it does from someone who has been, to my mind, wrongly branded a 'regional' writer. My first experience of Renu was through the film whose haunting lyrics and strong screenplay were etched indelibly upon my mind. Then came the TV adaptation of 'Panchlight', which spurred me to scout for more such stories of rural India that could speak to me—entirely city-bred though I was—with vividness and clarity.

Years ago, I translated *Aatm-Sakshi* (literally meaning 'Self-Testimony', which has been included here as simply 'The Testimony'). I recall the thrill of discovering something that was at once so inexplicably real and hence so immediate, despite being grounded in a milieu that was completely alien to me. That thrill has endured; it has stayed with me as I chanced upon story after story that had, on the one hand, characters and locations steeped in Bihar (a state which, incidentally, I have never visited and am therefore not familiar with at first hand), yet beckoned me—first as a reader and, later, as a translator—to look for the known and the familiar. The more I read, the more this duality grew till in a strange way it resolved itself, as I slowly realised that for a good writer, character, plot and narration are mere props; the real thing is the story and, in the telling of it, if the writer can perchance touch the reader at some level—be it emotional or intellectual—then the remoteness of its setting or the strangeness of its characters is of little consequence.

This collection of ten stories is an attempt to share the sense of wonder that Renu has unfailingly evoked in me. Increasingly, I began to feel that Renu has the almost uncanny power to hold his reader by the hand and take him/her into a world that is hidden deep within the vast hinterland of India—a dark world of abject poverty, ignorance, helplessness, exploitation and superstition, but one that is also lit from within by translucent beams of life. The will to live, the zeal to carry on with dignity and grace, the inherent desire in human beings—no matter how lowly or brought low by fate and circumstance—to rise above the human condition, permeates these seemingly dark stories of lives that could have been wretched but are actually, and inexplicably, not so in the least.

Renu was a prolific writer; he wrote five short story collections, six novels, five books of reportage, three memoirs, and several biographical sketches and essays. In an autobiographical sketch called *Pandulekh*, he wrote, 'Whenever I have tried to write something about myself—the image of GBS (George Bernard Shaw) appears before me with irony in his eyes and a meaningful smile behind his beard. And my pen stops. It is impossible to write accurately about oneself... No one can do it.'[1] Maybe that is why he never wrote his autobiography. Renu held the truth above all else and the bulk of his writings testify to what he saw and believed. As a result, there is no artifice, no attempt to make reality subservient to politics or political correctness, or to twist and turn situations to suit an ideology.

Renu actively participated in the freedom struggle, went to jail on several occasions and, after independence, supported peasants' movements and the popular land reforms movement for *Sampurna Kranti* (Total Revolution) launched by Lok Nayak Jayaprakash Narayan. Such was his commitment to the people's movement, and such, too, was the extent of his frustration with the government's apathy towards it, that he chose to return the Padma Shree conferred upon him by the central government in 1970. He participated in street processions, toured the remotest of villages, bore the brunt of lathi-charges and tear gas shells, and kept up a ceaseless vigil against corruption and injustice. He participated in a massive peasants' rally in Patna on 25 November 1949, along with scores of peasants from Purnea district. Much of what he saw and experienced at close quarters found its way into his stories and reportage. Similarly, the

[1] From Bharat Yayawar (ed.), *Renu Rachna Sanchayan*, New Delhi: Sahitya Akademi, 1998, p. 25. The same essay was also published in *Dharmyug*, November 1, 1964.

great famine of 1966 and the floods of 1975 compelled him to write bone-chillingly authentic stories.

❋

Almost each one of the stories in this collection presents a cameo of defeat and despair followed by redemption and recovery. In story after story the redemption comes from the cavernous depths of the human heart. Renu believed that no matter how low a man might fall, he will rise one day, just as surely as the seed sprouts from the bosom of the earth.

In 'Old Story, New Moral', as village upon village is devastated by the fury of rives in full spate, the misery of man and beast is compounded by a corrupt-to-the-core state machinery and by short-sighted greed and self-interest. Yet new life bursts forth just as surely as a new seed puts out tentative new leaves and stems, which push their way out of the earth and find a place for themselves under the sun. For Renu, the coming of the floods is an old story; its new moral or lesson lies in present-day politics, which is infested by politicians who turn even human misery to their advantage.

'The Party's Ghost' is a tongue-in-cheek satire on the inevitable and unending politicisation of virtually every walk of life in the volatile society of the politically-charged state of Bihar. With everyone necessarily having to belong to one camp or the other, the Common Man, no matter how self-avowedly apolitical he might be, willy-nilly gets identified with a group or party (sometimes more than one party at the same time!), with hilarious and sometimes not-so-funny consequences. The perils of people polarised in warring camps; the tendency to view the other camp or party as the enemy; the predisposition to think along party lines instead of using one's own head; the appetite for petty power politics fuelled by a process that begins in schools, takes root in campuses and grows like a parasite feeding off the worst excesses of bias and prejudice; the proclivity for putting people into neat pigeonholes of this or that group; the propensity to indulge in the worst sort of regional chauvinism (such as Bengali vs Bihari)—all these come in for some good-natured scuffing. Renu sees the folly of such short-sighted alignments; by treating it in a light-hearted manner, he shows how ridiculous this sort of party politics is.

But the satire is sharper and the wit no longer droll in a subject closer to Renu's heart, that is, the eroding of people's faith in grassroots movements. 'The Testimony' is a bitter, clear-sighted and very insightful denouement of a failed system of party politics evident in the mother of all parties, the Left Party, which seized the imagination of the most downtrodden, disenfranchised and disempowered of India's rural poor by its big talk of justice and equality for all. The story is a candid account of the party's internal functioning, especially at the grassroots, using activists closest to the land and its people, and employing resources and techniques that, while broadly within the party's framework, were actually tailored to reach the Indian masses. But like all good things that come to an early end, the early successes of the party are tainted by corruption, greed, selfishness and petty politics.

Grassroots workers like Ganpat, who have, literally, devoted their entire life to selfless party work, are left feeling as faded and frazzled as the party flag that flutters uselessly in the wake of intra-party warfare. Comrade Ganpat, who once fasted and picketed and sang rousing songs like '*The sun is rising/ The red, red sun/ Wake, O peasant, wake/ Wake, O labouring brother, wake...*' and worked tirelessly for the peasants' movement and set up the 'Peasant Martyrs Ashram' is, in the end, caught between warring dissidents who measure success in terms of the donations collected during fund-raising drives. The testimony to his good work and good character, for what it is worth, comes from the people themselves, but it is too little, too late. Ganpat's sad plight mirrors the debacle of the people's movement that once had many young liberals in its thrall, including the younger and less cynical Renu himself.

Several stories depict a society poised precariously on the brink of change—there is a lot from the old way of life still left to document but everywhere there are ominous signs that these scenes and these people will soon be gone and the face of India's villages—where, according to Mahatma Gandhi, the 'real India' lived—will change irrevocably. It is to Renu's credit that he captures all this without being either overtly judgmental or grossly sentimental. 'The Wrestler's Drum', 'The Messenger' and 'Panchlight' show, in different ways, a crumbling social order and a rapidly-changing landscape. In 'The Wrestler's Drum', a former wrestler plays the drum to keep the spirit of a village alive during an epidemic in which people are dropping dead like flies.

'The Estrangement' is a nuanced story of a man's near-heroic escape from the clutches of the village moneylender and his return to the village and the life he had once fled in abject misery. The Bilaswa of yore returns from the city, where he had been plying the rickshaw and earning money while seeing a bit of the world and its ways, with a new name and identity. He is now Rambilas Singh, man about town. But, for all his new and hard-won confidence, he returns to whispers of marital infidelity.

Rambilas' wife, Jhumki, has learnt to fend for herself in his absence, even if it means taking a little help from Shivdhari, another landless peasant, who tends her buffalo and her crops, and harbours sweet dreams about her. Jhumki, like several other women in Renu's stories, is a strong, self-aware woman, not above using her charms to get what she wants, just like Birju's mother in 'The Queen of Hearts', who takes charge of her life in a clear-headed way when her husband shows signs of dithering. Renu's women are like the proverbial 'earth mothers'—real and rooted to the soil, nurturing, life-giving, and very hardy.

I have chosen to include 'Splendour' in this collection for two reasons: one, it is one of the few 'city' stories and shows the urbane, city-smart side of Renu, based as it is in Patna; and two, it has a Muslim woman as its main protagonist, which is rarer still. Despite living in an area with a mixed population, and for all his liberal, left leanings, it is odd that a writer such as Renu should have very few Muslims, if not in the main cast, then at the very least, lower down in the list of *dramatis personae*, unlike, say, Premchand, who has delineated some memorable Muslim characters such as Chaudhry Itrat Ali in 'The Temple and the Mosque' and the two Awadhi noblemen in 'The Chess Players'. Fatima Di of 'Splendour' is a flat character; for all her fiery rhetoric and impassioned posturing, she is not a real, living woman. She is different and alien, and therefore worthy of Renu's admiration. In my eyes, if Renu has failed, it is here. He has failed to produce a single character from the 'other' community who is real and believable and as ordinary as the host of other characters he has so skilfully and convincingly brought to life. It saddens me that a writer of Renu's calibre, and moreover living in a state with a large Muslim population, should have remained so untouched by a community that lived in close proximity and shared the joys and sorrows, the seasons of plenty and want, the floods and famines, as also the greed and corruption, the vices and virtues that, like the passing of the seasons, are common to all.

Renu uses language as a living tool. He mixes standard Hindi with local dialect with generous dollops of mispronounced English and Hindi words, such as *daghdar* for 'doctor', *lasaince* for 'licence', *dalaivery* for 'drivery' (not even a real English word but a Hindi derivative actually!), as befitting the rural, uneducated village characters, many of whom have never set food outside their own villages, while some others—the slightly more risque and adventurous characters—are the ones who travel by train (remember Bihar had a fairly extensive rail network), and the remaining few, the true sophisticates, are the ones who have been to Patna and can live off the 'Patna stories' for the rest of their lives. Sometimes, the characters knowingly use English words, though pronounced in such a peculiar fashion, with their syllables contorted so out of shape to fit the rhythms of the local dialect as to be unrecognisable, while at other times they use English words that are as incomprehensible and alien as the ideology they couch. In 'The Testimony' a new-breed 'comrade' tries to impress the rustic grassroots party activist with high-sounding English words he can barely comprehend, let alone pronounce: Illiterate Balram used to pepper his speech with many English words like capitalist, bourgeois, proletariat, reactionary, and many more.' Then there are the other common English words, so common in fact that they have been appropriated as native with a few minor alterations, such as *chheent* for 'chintz', *teeshun* for 'station', *malaitary* for 'military', *sarbay sittalminty* for 'survey settlement', *t-sart* for 't-shirt' and so on. There are others such as mill, drama, part (sometimes pronounced *palt*), torch (almost always pronounced *tarch*), suitcase, survey camp and, of course, the omnipresent 'party', used freely and frequently even by those from the remote hinterland.

Apart from this highly individualistic use of English, there is also the liberal use of the local dialect, called Angik, which is spoken in the Kathiar, Purnea and Araria districts. The Hindi original of Renu's stories are at once melodious and mystifying. While the frequent use of onomatopoeic sounds—big bells around bullocks go *jhunur-jhunur* but the smaller bells around goats go *tunur-tunur*, or the wrestler's drum that speaks in a myriad tongues—leaven the narrative with notes from a strange but not altogether displeasing melody, there is plenty here that makes the Hindi reader draw a blank. I have, on numerous occasions, taken the help of friends and acquaintances from Bihar, particularly from the Kathiar region, to decipher the more idiomatic expressions, such as *na aage nath na peeche paghiya* that refers to the nose ring and tail rope of a bullock's harness. Then there are the folk songs that are virtually untranslatable, yet are so very magical. Renu has a penchant for studding his narrative with snatches of songs and fragments of popular ballads. Sung by itinerant singers and professional bards, they leaven the text with the loamy smell of the soil that sprouted Renu and his true-to-life characters.

Trains and railway tracks make for a near-mythic element in Renu's writing and Kathiar junction is almost a totemic character in some stories. Trains are mentioned in many roundabout ways—characters travel in them, live beside their tracks, or set up shops and small businesses close to stations. The *Teeshun Babu* (Station Master) is invariably a good sort, an upright fellow, though his underlings such as the godown-keepers are often corrupt or derelict in their duties. Renu uses the railways as a means to convey the depth and extent of the changes that were already knocking at the door of rural India by the middle of the twentieth century. In his characteristically non-judgmental way, he doesn't blame the railways for introducing these changes; he simply sees it as an agent of change which is, inevitably, both good and bad. In 'The Queen of Hearts', Jangi's young daughter-in-law, who has grown up close to the station, is brash and outspoken. She speaks her mind and is unafraid of the other village women, even those who are better off than her. She knows all the latest songs. She brings with her a whiff of change and is viewed with suspicion by the other village women. She is the '*teeshunwali*'.

Elsewhere, trains are both the agent of change and the emblem of changing times and social mores. The easy mobility they provide is a far cry from a time when people seldom traveled outside their villages. The Araria of Renu's birth had remained caught in a time warp, largely untouched by the outside world. As power slipped and changed hands from warring tribes to Rajput chieftains to nawabs and rajahs and thence to the British, till finally it landed in the laps of home-grown *neta*s and *mantri*s, the fate of Araria remained of little consequence to the world at large. Yet, this area beside the river Kosi, home to Renu and his forefathers, is a primeval land. Several ancient tribes, such as the Angas, Kiratas and Pundras who inhabited these parts, find mention in the Vedas. Araria continued to find mention in tracts dating to the Maurya and Gupta periods. The Chinese traveler, Huein Tsang, who visited this area in AD 640, mentions a flourishing population and a land studded with tanks, hospices and flowering groves. The land, he records, was low-lying and humid, with abundant crops and a genial climate.

Till the late twelfth century, when Bakhtiyar Khilji trampled through Bihar on his onward march to Bengal, Araria remained untouched by Muslim influence. It was only in the eighteenth century that control over this fertile land, watered by many small rivers, was finally wrested from the northern tribes. It was in the year 1738 that the military governor of Purnea, Nawab Saif Khan, son of an Afghan Amir, recovered the area north of the Jalalgarh fort up to Jogbani (i.e., the present Araria district) from the Rajput kings of Morung, and thence began Araria's brush with Muslim rule. Till today, Araria and Purnea districts continue to have large population of Muslims, who number over a million. Hence my worry about Renu's near-blindness to their presence seems all the more alarming.

Where Renu cannot be faulted, however, is in his championing of the landless peasants, who toiled on the land they had sprung from, yet could not stake any claim to; they were, and are, the real underdogs of rural India. Renu took up cudgels on their behalf, both as a political activist and as a writer. He told their stories, and told them well, because he knew their plight better than most. Whether it is Sirchan of 'The Hurt' or Bilaswa *aka* Rambilas Singh of 'The Estrangement', Renu never deviated from his clear understanding that those who toil the most—the landless peasant and the village artisan, who own little or no land—occupy the lowest rung in the socio-economic ladder and form the class that is the worst off in rural India.

New Delhi
August 2009

Rakhshanda Jalil

The Wrestler's Drum

A winter's night. And a moonless one too—cold and dark. The malaria and cholera-ridden village shivered like a frightened child. The twin powers of darkness and silence ruled over the cluster of bedraggled desolate bamboo huts. Darkness and stillness.

The dark night shed silent tears. The stillness tried desperately hard to bury the piteous sighs and sobs in its bosom. Stars twinkled in the sky above. But on the earth there was no trace of light. If perchance some sentimental star thought of falling out of the sky to the earth below, its light would dissipate somewhere on the way. And the other stars in the firmament would laugh out loud at its mawkish ineptitude.

The frightening howls and cries of jackals occasionally pierced the stillness, as did the intermittent sounds of people vomiting or groaning inside their huts. The now imploring, now high-pitched cries of 'Hare Ram!' and 'Hey Bhagwan!' broke out from within. A child somewhere feebly cried out 'Ma! Ma!', then fell silent. But none of these sounds had any significant impact on the implacable stillness of the night.

Dogs have a special instinct for sensing a situation. All day long they would lie atop heaps of rubbish with their tails tucked in and bodies coiled in a tight bundle. But in the dense darkness of the night, they would howl in unison.

And so the night progressed, intense and still, and the only sound that challenged its intensity was the beat of the wrestler's drum. From dusk to dawn it beat with the same unwavering tempo—'*Chat-dha, gid-dha,... Chat-dha, gid-dha!*' as though saying: 'Come on, fight me, come on, fight me!' Sometimes, the beat would change to say: '*Chatak-chat-dha,... Chatak-chat-dha!*' implying 'Pick-and-toss, pick-and-toss!'

This sound worked as a miracle drug—*sanjivani*—infusing fresh life into the dying village.

Luttan Singh, the wrestler! He was fond of declaring that the 'whole' of India had heard of him, but, perhaps, his definition of the 'whole' of India was restricted to his own district, for the people of his district knew him well enough.

Luttan had lost his parents when he was a lad of nine. Fortunately, he had already been married off, or he too would have gone his parents' way. His widowed mother-in-law raised him. He grazed cattle, drank gallons of milk and exercised vigorously. He had begun the exercising and body-building initially to protect his widowed mother-in-law from the harassment of the villagers and later to take revenge on them. Regular physical training from early youth had made his chest and arms strong and muscular. By the time he stepped into early manhood, he was considered the finest and fittest wrestler in his village. People began to be in awe of him and he took to strutting around the village, like a wrestler with his arms akimbo, at a 45° angle to his body. He also began to wrestle and joust regularly.

One day he went to watch a wrestling match at the fair in nearby Shyamnagar. Watching the wrestlers grapple and wrestle and try out tricks and stratagems, he could no longer contain himself. The headiness of youth and the throbbing insistent beat of the drums inside the wrestlers' arena caused an uncontrollable excitement to run through his veins. Without pausing to consider the outcome of his action, he challenged the undisputed reigning king of the arena, the 'Lion's Cub' no less!

The real name of 'Lion's Cub' was Chand Singh. He had come to the fair at Shyamnagar for the first time with his mentor, the wrestler Badal Singh, all the way from Punjab. A beautiful young man, good health and good looks dripped from every pore of his body. In a matter of three days he had defeated the Pathan wrestlers and others from Punjab as well as all the young men from the neighbouring districts, who had been foolish enough to take him on, and won the title of 'Lion's Cub'. Now he trotted around the arena, wearing nothing but a loincloth, sniggering and laughing. Even the thought of engaging him in combat petrified the village youth. To live up to his name, Chand Singh would let out a mighty roar from time to time.

The ageing ruler of Shyamnagar and the sport-loving patron of the fair, was thinking of installing Chand Singh at his court as the royal protégé, when Luttan chose to challenge the 'Lion's Cub'. At first the feted and lionised Chand Singh was taken aback at this temerity, then he smiled at such competition. He pounced like a falcon falling upon its prey.

Excitement ran through the so far silent crowd of spectators. 'Madness!...He's mad!...He'll get himself killed!' But what a brave lad Luttan turned out to be! With such cleverness he escaped unscathed from the powerful attack and began to show his own deft moves. Raja Sahab had the bout stopped, called Luttan aside and tried to talk sense into him. He praised the boy's courage, handed him a ten-rupee note and said, 'Go, see the fair, and go home.'

'No, my lord, I will fight, just give me permission...'

'You are mad, boy, go home...'

Everyone from the Raja's manager to the sentries tried to dissuade him; 'You don't have an ounce of flesh on your body and you are going to take on the Lion's Cub? His Highness is trying his best to make you understand, and you...'

'Forgive me, Your Highness, I will dash my head against a rock and give up my life…please, please allow me to fight!' he pleaded with folded hands.

The crowd grew restive. The drums had fallen silent. Mad with rage, the pack of Punjabi wrestlers was flinging the choicest abuses at Luttan. Those who had come to see this unusual match became increasingly vocal and exited. Every now and then a voice would cry out in Luttan's favour: 'Let him fight!…Let him fight!'

Chand Singh stood alone in the arena, trying valiantly to keep his smile in place. He had already got a taste of his opponent's strength in the very first tackle.

Finally, Raja Sahab had to give in. 'Let him fight,' he said.

The drums began to beat. Excitement coursed through the crowd. The noise and confusion increased. Shopkeepers began to close their shops and run towards the arena, shouting at one another: 'Chand Singh has found his match!…Hurry, let's go watch this bout!'

❧

'*Chat-dha, gid-dha, chat-dha, gid-dha...*'

A drum that had been silent all this while, spoke up in a bold, staccato voice:

'*Dhak-dhina, dhak-dhina, dhak-dhina...*'

(meaning 'Bravo-bravo, bravo-bravo, bravo-bravo…')

Chand held Luttan in a vice-like grip.

'Gone!' 'He's done for!' The crowd clapped, 'He'll be turned to pulp! He'll get pulverised! It's no joke—after all, he's not called the Lion's Cub for nothing.'

'*Chat-gid-dha, chat-gid-dha, chat-gid-dha...*'

('Never-fear, never-fear, never-fear...')

Chand was digging his elbow into Luttan's neck, inching him closer to the ground. 'Bury him, my brave boy, dig him into the earth!' Badal Singh exhorted his pupil.

Luttan's eyes were nearly popping out. His chest was ready to burst. The royalty as well as majority were united in opinion—both seemed clearly in Chand's favour. Everyone was egging him on. The only voice in Luttan's favour was the drum's, on whose beat he was testing his will power and prowess, and raising his strength to a crescendo. Suddenly, a falsetto emerged from the drum: '*Dhak-dhina, tirkat-tina, dhak-dhina, tirkat-tina…*!'

Luttan could clearly hear the drum say: 'Twist-and-out, twist-and-out...'

The crowd's surprise knew no bounds when Luttan twisted out of Chand's grip and caught him by the neck in a trice.

'What a fake Lion's Cub he turned out to be!'

He escaped his clutches, no wonder...' the crowd's opinion was clearly turning around.

Luttan tried a wily move and quickly brought Chand crashing down.

'*Dhik-dhina, dhik-dhina…*'

(Throw-him, Throw-him…')

Luttan tried one last time with all his strength and Chand lay spreadeagled on his back.

'*Dha-gid-gid, dha-gid-gid, dha-gid-gid...*' (My-brave-kid, my-brave-kid, my-brave-kid…')

Overcome with excitement the crowd couldn't quite decide how to cheer for the winner. So the sky was rent by mingled cries of 'Victory to Mother Durga!' and 'Victory to Lord Mahavir!' and 'Victory to Raja Shyamanand'. The last exultant hoop drowned all other cries.

Victorious Luttan ran towards the drummers, skipping and jumping with joy, leaping to the beat of the drums. He bowed his head in obeisance to the drums. Then he ran towards the Raja Sahab and plucked him in his arms, heedless of the mud soiling the expensive royal garments. The manager clucked 'Hey-Hey!…Arre-Arre!' But the Raja Sahab drew Luttan to his bosom and chuckled with pride, 'May you live long, my brave warrior! You have saved the honour of this land!'

The pack of wrestlers from Punjab was busy wiping Chand's tears. Raja Sahab not only showered Luttan with gifts but also kept him in his court for the rest of his life. From that day Luttan became the royal wrestler and Raja Sahab began to call him 'Luttan Singh'. The royal priests made a face and protested, 'My Lord, he's a cowherd by caste, how can we call him 'Singh…'

The manager belonged to the Kshatriya caste, the community of warriors. Screwing his clean-shaven face into a puckered ball, he was busy pulling out an offending hair from his nostril with all his might. Finally, when he had succeeded in pulling the hair out, he said, 'Yes, My Lord, this is most unfair...'

Raja Sahab merely smiled and said, 'He has done the job of a Kshatriya.'

From that day Luttan Singh's fame spread far and wide. A healthy diet, regular exercise and royal patronage added to his glory. Over the next few years he beat all the known and famous wrestlers of the area.

About Kala Khan it was said that the moment he put on his loincloth and pounced on his opponent with a shout of 'Ya-Ali'[1], the opponent was struck by paralysis. Luttan brought him down too and dispelled this long-held belief.

By now Luttan had become a cult figure—a living-breathing trophy to be 'shown-off' at the court. In the royal menagerie, when the caged beasts rattled their cage and roared, 'Haaa-ooo, Haaa-ooo…', those who heard the bellow rightly assumed, 'It is the lion's roar.'

[1] 'Ya Ali'—often used as an invocation to Ali, the Prophet's son-in-law, known to favour the brave in battle.

So also when the royal wrestler visited the Thakur's colony and roared 'Mahaa-Vir!'[2] every one understood it was the wrestler calling.

Luttan would show up at village fairs—clad in a robe that barely reached his knees, and a haphazardly tied turban on his head—roaming about like an intoxicated elephant. Shopkeepers would call out to seek his custom. The vendor of sweets would say, 'Fresh *rasgulla*s have been made, come and try some.'

And the wrestler would gurgle like a happy child and say, 'Why some? Bring me a *ser* and a half!'

After gorging the *rasgullas* and stuffing eight or ten *paan*s in his mouth, the red betel juice dribbling down his chin, he would set out once again on his leisurely, unhurried round of the fair. By the time he returned to the court, his appearance would be strangely transformed: on his eyes he would have a child's coloured-paper goggles, in his hand a twirling dinky toy and in his mouth a brass whistle; he would be gay and carefree as a child returning after a fun-filled day at the fair. As his strength and body grew, his intelligence diminished to that of a child's.

But as soon as he entered the wrestler's arena and heard the drums beat, he would begin to flaunt and parade his well-built muscular body. He could hardly ever find someone willing to take him on, and on the rare occasion that someone did come along, Raja Sahab would forbid him from competing. And so, the disappointed wrestler, wearing a loincloth, his body smeared with mud, would strut around like a prize bull or stud. And the old Raja Sahab would look on and smile fondly.

[2] Literally meaning, 'very brave', it is also a title for Hanuman, the Monkey God, brave lieutenant in Lord Ram's army and patron saint of wrestlers in India.

Fifteen years passed in this manner. The wrestler remained unvanquished. Now he would enter the arena with his two grown-up sons. His mother-in-law had died a long time ago; his wife had given birth to two stud-like sons and gone to heaven. The two boys were strong and powerfully built like their father. People who saw them in the arena would exclaim, 'These two will be even greater than their father!'

The boys had already been declared the future royal protégés. Hence, their food and drink were supplied by the royal coffers. Every morning, the father would beat the drum himself and supervise their training. In the afternoon, he would lie down and instruct them about worldly matters: 'Keep your attention focused on the drum beats. Understand! No wrestler has been my teacher; it is the drum that has taught me everything. Understand! I have become a wrestler due to the power of the drum. When you enter the arena, you must first bow your head in obeisance to the drum. Understand!...' And he would go on in similar fashion. He would also tell his sons how to keep the royal master happy, how to behave and deport themselves in the court, and so on and so forth.

But one fine day all his hard work and teachings came to naught. The aged ruler died. The prince, newly arrived from foreign lands, took over the reins of the kingdom. The flabbiness that had accumulated during the old king's times was now quickly dissipated. Many changes were brought about. The wrestler became a victim of these changes. Horse racing took the place of wrestling bouts.

The prince heard of the amount spent on feeding the wrestler's sons and exclaimed, 'Terrible!'

The new manager said, 'Horrible!'

The wrestler was informed in no uncertain terms: there was no position for him at the court. He was not even given the time to plead.

That very day he set off for his village accompanied by his two sons and his drum slung from one shoulder. In his village the villagers put up a shack at one end of the village and the wrestler began to live there. He started training the village lads and cowherds. The villagers took care of his meals. Every morning and evening the wrestler would beat the drum himself and teach the fine points of wrestling, its twists and turns and stratagems to his sons and the village youth.

❦

The sons of poor peasants and labourers had barely enough to fill their own bellies, so where would they find the sort of food that a wrestler needs! Gradually people stopped corning. Finally, the wrestler was left with his two sons whom he taught tactics and manoeuvres to the beat of the drum. The two sons would take on casual work in the course of the day and the three managed to survive on whatever little they earned.

Till, suddenly, the village was struck by calamity. First drought, then food shortages, then malaria and, finally, cholera devastated the villagers.

The village wore a deserted look. Rows upon rows of homes began to empty out. Two or three corpses were taken away daily. Panic reigned. During the day some signs of life could be seen on people's faces despite the wailing and weeping—or perhaps it was the light of the sun that made it seem so. As soon as the sun came up, people would come out of their homes—coughing and groaning and sighing—visit the homes of neighbours and friends and say encouraging things. 'Come on now, stop crying. He had to go, so he has gone. Look after those who are left behind.'

'Brother, how long will you keep the dead in your home and cry over his body?'

'Shroud? What need is there for a shroud? Put him in the river.'

But as soon as the sun had set, they would creep into their huts and not let out so much as a squeak. As the night progressed, it was as though their powers of speech too ebbed away. Mothers didn't have the strength to call out one last time to their dying sons who lay beside them.

It was only the wrestler's drum that could hurl defiance at the terror of the night. From dusk till dawn, regardless of the reasons why the wrestler beat his drum, its sound worked like the magic drug *sanjivani* on the half-dead denizens of the village, suffering without recourse to medicine or doctor or wholesome diet. Scenes from the wrestling arena would begin to dance in front of the eyes of the children, youth and the elderly. Throbbing, quivering, pulsating energy would begin to course through enfeebled nerves and sinews like lightning. Undoubtedly, the sound of the drum in itself had neither the power to check the unbridled spread of the dreaded disease nor any special aptitude to make the fever go away, but there was no denying the fact that it could make the dying close their eyes peacefully; it could make the fear of death go away.

The day the heartless hour struck for the wrestler's sons, the boys cried out, 'Father, play that "pick-and-throw" tune!'

'*Chatak-chat-dha, Chatah-chat-dha...*' all night the wrestler beat his drum. Every now and then he would exhort his sons in the language of a true wrestler, 'Beat him, throw him, my brave ones!'

Early in the morning he saw his sons lying motionless on the ground. They lay flat on their bellies. One had even dug up a bit of loose dirt with his teeth. The wrestler took a deep breath and tried to smile, 'The two brave boys have fallen.'

Then he wore the satin shorts given to him by King Shyamanand. He rubbed mud all over his body, did some sit-ups, carried his sons' bodies to the river and put them in the water. When the people heard this, they were shocked. Many despaired and lost heart.

But come night and the sound of the wrestler's drum could be heard as always. It consoled and reassured them. Many a grief-stricken father and mother said, 'Look at the wrestler, he has lost both his sons, but he's still bearing up. What amazing fortitude!'

Four or five days passed. One night the sound of the drum was not heard. The drum didn't speak to the villagers.

A few of the wrestler's brave but ailing disciples went to check on him and found his corpse lying spreadeagled on the ground. Jackals had torn off chunks from the wrestler's well-muscled thigh. And from the stomach too...

They wiped their tears and one of them said, 'He always used to say that when I die, lay me down on my stomach, not flat on my back. I have never been thrown flat on my back. And when you light my pyre, play the drum for me.' He could speak no more.

The drum lay rolled over beside the body. The jackals had torn away its leather covering.

The Hurt

At harvest time, when every hand is needed, Sirchan is not among those counted as able-bodied men. He is regarded as not just 'useless', but also 'unusable'. And that is why no one ever comes to call Sirchan to pitch in for seasonal work. What's the point of calling him, after all? When all the other landless labourers have reached the fields and are almost one-thirds through the work, Sirchan Rai will deign to show up, dangling a hoe from one hand, tiptoeing among the fields as though he has all the time in the world. If someone is giving away wages for free, then it is another matter!

Today you can call Sirchan a good-for-nothing and ever-hungry freeloader, but there was a time when the door to his house was crowded with wagons and carriages of the rich and powerful. He was not just popular but also much sought after… 'Dear Brother Sirchan, you are the only one in the entire district who still has a pair of gifted hands. You have to take some time out and come to my house. My elder brother has written from the city; he has asked for a set of wicker blinds made by you.'

I remember that whenever my mother would want to send for Sirchan, my first question would be, 'And what are you going to give him to eat?'

Mother would laugh and say, 'Stop making fun of poor Sirchan! He never raises the question of food when I ask him to do something for me.'

Once, in front of my own eyes, Sirchan had so embarrassed the younger son of Panchand Chaudhry of the Brahmin Colony: 'Your sister-in-law serves no more vegetables than what she can scrape out with her fingernail. And I always thought it is us lowly types who make *kadhi* with tamarind pulp instead of curd; where did your sister-in-law learn to make it like that?'

And so I always thought it best to ask my mother before calling Sirchan…

Mother would take one look at Sirchan and say cheerfully, 'There you are, Sirchan! Nenu was churning the butter, and I thought of calling you. You love *chewra* with *ghee*, don't you? By the way, my elder daughter has sent a message from her in-laws' house. Her sister-in-law absolutely insists on a rush mat that only you can make.'

Sirchan would attempt to smile through his watering mouth and lolling tongue, and say, 'Kaki, I smelt the sweet aroma of *ghee* and came straightaway. Otherwise, there isn't a moment's respite in this season of weddings and festivities.'

Sirchan is an artisan by caste. I have sat for hours and watched him work. He gathers every strand of *mothi* and thread and makes a fine broom-like object. Then, he spends practically an entire day dyeing this broom and untangling the skein of loose threads. If someone disturbs him at work, he hisses at them like a hooded snake: 'Go and get your work done by someone else!' Sirchan is loudmouthed, but not lazy. He is the sort of man who can do a full day's work without wages, as long as he is given enough rice to fill his belly. He will work for you even if you don't indulge his sweet tooth, but if you don't use a sweet tongue while dealing with him, he won't work for you.

There are many who consider him a greedy glutton… Tasty, fried vegetables, *kadhi* made from curd, milk topped with layers of cream—if you have arranged for all this, then you can call Sirchan and he will come wagging his tail! If there is the slightest laxity in the milk-cream-*ghee* quotient, watch his work become lax. He will leave his work half-finished and get up saying, 'I have a terrible migraine; I will come back another day and finish it.' 'Another day' usually meant 'never'.

Colourful mats woven out of dyed thread and *mothi* reeds, shimmering *chik*s made with spliced bamboo shoots, brightly coloured stools made out of multi-hued cords, huge nets and hanging baskets made by twisting and weaving coir and rope, plates and cups fashioned from dried leaves and countless other objects of daily use—Sirchan is the only one in the village who can make all this and more. It is another matter that now these things are considered useless trifles for which Sirchan need not be paid either money or wheat. Give him enough to fill his belly, hand him an old set of clothes once the job is done and send him on his way; he won't say anything…

It is not true that he won't say anything. Those who have gone to call Sirchan know well enough that Sirchan is an artist with words as well. Once, Bhajju Mahajan's daughter, who lived in the merchants' colony, got a mouthful from Sirchan and ran off in a huff, saying: 'I shall go and tell my mother! How dare you make such a big thing out of it?'

Sirchan smiled and said, 'It is true, *bitiya*, that only big people can do or say big things! Or else, how could your mother have expected me to make such a huge matting for her for a handful of *sattu*. Only your mother would think of doing it, child.'

❋

My youngest sister was about to leave our home for her new, married home. She would be leaving us for the very first time. Her husband had already written to our elder sister-in-law and warned her: 'I don't care if you don't send boxes of sweets with Manu, but if you send her without three sets of fashionable bamboo *chik*s and two rush mats, then…' My sister-in-law had laughingly answered: 'Return to sender!'

Mother had sent for Sirchan two weeks in advance and put him to work, saying, 'Look here, Sirchan, I will give you a new *dhoti* this time, a real mill-made *dhoti*, with a real stamp on it. Put all your heart and soul into it and make something really spectacular this time—something that is sure to dazzle all those who see it.'

Sirchan set to work splicing slivers of bamboo and splitting reeds and twigs with his razor-sharp knife. Spools of brightly coloured thread ran through the curtain of twigs as he sat down to weave. With barely a foot or so of the *chik* ready, everyone agreed that this time Sirchan was creating something new, something that no one had ever seen before.

My middle sister-in-law could no longer contain her envy. She spoke up from behind the curtain, 'Had I known that a mill-made *dhoti* could spur you to produce such goods, I would have written to my brother to send one long ago!'

Engrossed in his work, Sirchan heard these words and said, 'A silk kurta along with a mill-made *dhoti* cannot produce such work, *bahuriya*. Manu Didi is Kaki's youngest daughter... and Manu Didi's groom is a big-shot officer in the city!'

My middle sister-in-law was suitably abashed. My aunt whispered, 'Why are you wasting your time talking to him? It is not the prospect of the mill-made *dhoti*, but that of *laddoo*s made out of *moong dal,* that is producing this fine work! He will get to eat sweets everyday when the youngest daughter of the household is going away. You wait and see!'

By the next day, we could discern a pattern of seven twinkling stars in the intricate mesh of the bamboo curtain—each in a different colour. When Sirchan is deeply engrossed in his work, his tongue peeps out and rests on his slightly open lips. At such times, he forgets to eat or drink. He ran the warp of a long piece of twine through the weft of the bamboo twigs and turned to glance at the straw basket kept nearby. The basket had a handful of *chewra* and a lump of dry *gur*. I could see two frown lines appear on either side of Sirchan's nose. I ran to mother and said, 'Who has given the food to Sirchan; there is only *chewra* and *gur*.'

Mother was busy cooking snacks for the guests. She said, 'I can't be expected to see to everything.' Then calling out to my middle sister-in-law she said, 'Why hasn't Sirchan been given the *boondi laddoos*?'

'I don't eat *boondi*, Kaki.' Sirchan spoke through a mouthful of *chewra*. The lump of *gur* remained untouched in the basket.

Meanwhile, my middle sister-in-law heard mother's reprimand and got thoroughly piqued. She stormed off to dump a fistful of *boondi* in the straw basket beside Sirchan.

Sirchan drank some water and said, 'Do you distribute the sweets sent by your family with the same open-handed generosity?'

That was enough to make my middle sister-in-law lock herself in her room and burst into tears. My aunt came to my mother and added fuel to the fire. 'These people from the low castes have a low thinking. If you give them an inch, they take a mile. You talk sweetly to them and they think they can be free with us. How dare he talk about what someone's family has sent or not sent?'

My middle sister-in-law was mother's favourite daughter-in-law. Duly enraged, mother came out and said, 'Sirchan, you have come here to work, so concentrate on your work. There is no need to bandy words with the daughters-in-law of this house. If you want something, ask me.'

Sirchan went red in the face. He gave no answer. Then he turned towards the incomplete bamboo curtain and once again began to loop the threads through it.

Manu was preparing a tray of *paan* to send to the men's sitting-room. She handed a folded *paan* to Sirchan and said quietly, 'Sirchan Dada, you can see there is so much work to be done in this house. There are all kinds of people and they will say all kinds of things. Don't pay heed to anything people here might say to you.'

Sirchan smiled and put the *paan* in his mouth. At that very moment, my aunt was coming out of her room. She saw Sirchan eating *paan* and flew into a rage. Sirchan, for his part, saw my aunt staring angrily at him and decided to provoke her by saying, 'Chhoti Chachi, give me a little of your special scented tobacco. It has been so long...'

My aunt could never stand Sirchan. She would never have found a better occasion to vent her spleen at him. Now, she hissed, 'You think you can joke with me? May your lolling tongue catch fire! How dare you eat *paan* inside the house and ask for scented tobacco, you greedy pig!'

My heart sank. We were in for big trouble.

The cord tied itself in loops around Sirchan's limp fingers. For a few minutes he sat motionless, with the *paan* dissolving in his mouth. Then he got up abruptly and went to spit the betel juice in the backyard. He returned and began to gather his tools—the knives and blades and sickles—and put them away in his cloth bag. He looked once at the incomplete bamboo curtain hanging from its peg and charged out of the door.

My aunt muttered, 'What a temper! We are not getting work done for nothing; a mill-made *dhoti* costs eight rupees. The scoundrel has no control over his tongue, or his manners. You can buy scores of better *chik*s, if you have the money to spend. Women from the Bantar Colony go around selling stacks of these blinds.'

Manu remained silent. She kept staring wordlessly at the incomplete *chik* hanging from its peg in the verandah... the seven glittering stars had dimmed.

Mother said, 'Let it be, Manu. Don't let it bother you. I will buy some from the market and send with you.'

Manu remembered the rush mat made by Sirchan that mother had sent at the time of her wedding. Her in-laws had unrolled it and shown it so proudly to the guests from Calcutta and Patna. Manu got up and went to our elder sister-in-law's room.

I rushed off to mollify Sirchan. I found him lying on a tattered rush mat, deep in thought. He saw me and said, 'Babuaji! Not any more! I hold my ears and swear, never again... What will I do with a mill-made *dhoti*? Who's there to wear it? My wife died and took my sons and daughters along. Had my wife been alive today, Babuaji, would I have known such misfortune? She had woven this mat. I touch this mat and swear I will never do this work again… Yours was the only house in the entire village where my work was respected, where *I* was respected… And now?'

I returned silently. I could understand that an artist's feelings had been hurt. He couldn't come with me anymore.

Our elder sister-in-law stitched a frill of gaily-patterned chintz on the incomplete *chik*. 'It doesn't look too bad now, does it Manu?'

Manu didn't say a word. Poor thing, what could she say? But I couldn't remain quiet. I said, 'Watch out that it doesn't catch the eye of our aunt and middle sister-in-law! They will soon put a jinx on this too!'

I was supposed to accompany Manu on her journey to her new home.

When the luggage was being checked at the railway platform, Manu was found clutching the incomplete *chik*. Anger welled up inside me. I felt like heaping all those abuses at Sirchan that our aunt had flung at him—lazy, good-for-nothing, greedy guts!

The train pulled in. I loaded the luggage and was shutting the door when I spotted Sirchan running on the platform. 'Babuaji!' he shouted as he came close to the door of my compartment.

'What is it?' I asked gruffly, peering through the bars of my window. Sirchan lowered a bundle from his back and looked at me. 'I have come running all the way… Open the door. Where is Manu Didi? Let me see her one last time.'

I opened the door.

'Sirchan Dada!' Manu could say no more.

Sirchan stood on the platform beside our window and stuttered, 'This is from my side. Everything is there, Didi—the rush mats, *chiks* and a pair of low stools made from *kush* grass.'

The train began to move. Manu tried to give him the money for a mill-made *dhoti*. But Sirchan stopped her with folded hands, shaking his head and tutting with his tongue bitten between his teeth.

Manu was crying like a baby. I opened the bundle and began to examine its contents. Such fine craftsmanship, such intricacy, such delicate threading of the coloured cord through the bamboo slats—no one had ever seen anything like this.

Panchlight

The elders of Mahto Toli bought a petromax at this year's Ramnavmi fair from the fines and penalties collected over the past fifteen months. There are eight panchayats in the village, one for each community. All the panchayats have their own *durries, jajim,* mats and a petromax lamp, which the villagers call Panchlight.

After buying the Panchlight, the panchayat members decided to buy offerings for *puja* with the ten rupees that were left over, for it would be most inappropriate to use a technical object with nuts and bolts without first having it suitably blessed. After all, even in the time of the British Bahadur, a sacrifice would be offered to appease the gods before work could begin on building a bridge.

All the panchayat members returned home from the fair well before sunset—the orderly in front carrying the box with the Panchlight on his head, followed by the chief, the secretary and the other members. Phutangi Jha of the Brahmin Toli stopped them at the outskirts of the village and asked, 'How much did you buy this lantern for?'

'Can't you see? This is a Panchlight! You people from the Brahmin Toli think no end of yourselves. You will call the flickering oil lamp in your home an electric bulb and when someone else buys a Panchlight, it looks like a lantern to you!'

By the time they reached their own *toli,* word had spread. Every one dropped whatever they were doing and rushed to see the Panchlight. 'Come on, come on. Hurry! Our Panchlight has come!'

The orderly, Agnu Mahto, kept issuing stern warnings: 'Watch out! Don't come too close! Don't touch it! See you don't damage it!'

The chief of the Panchayat told his wife: 'There will be *a puja* in the evening. Hurry up and cook my dinner, and you too take a bath and get ready.'

The head of the neighbourhood troupe of singers told his musicians: 'Look here, tonight we shall be performing in the light of the Panchlight. So all you out-of-tune types better watch out! One false note and you are out!'

Gulri Kaki, one of the leading lights of the women's choir, began to hum. Little boys and girls started a ruckus, shouting and crying for no reason save uncontrollable excitement.

There was still an hour to go before sunset, but people had already gathered at the chief's door. The chant went up: 'Panchlight! Panchlight!'

There was no other topic for either conversation or gossip, except the Panchlight. The chief gurgled on his *hukkah* and said, 'The shopkeeper asked for five cowries and five rupees. I said, "Don't take me for an ignorant rustic; I have seen lots of Panchlights." At first, the shopkeeper could only gape at me. Then he said, "Looks like you are a chief by caste! All right, since the chief himself has come to my shop to buy a Panchlight, I will charge only five cowries for it."'

The secretary of the Panchayat added: 'That shopkeeper could read faces. The shop's servant didn't want to give us a box for the Panchlight, but I said, "Mr Shopkeeper, how can we carry the Panchlight without its box?" The shopkeeper scolded his servant and said, "What is this? Are you trying to fool the secretary? Give him the box."'

The people from the *toli* looked at the chief and the secretary with new respect. The orderly was telling a crowd of women, 'It was making funny noises all the way—*sannn-sannn*...'

But… at the precise moment a 'but' reared its ugly head. Three bottles of kerosene had been fetched from Rudal Sah's shop, but now the question was: 'Who would light the Panchlight?'

No one had thought of it so far. No one had thought of it before buying the Panchlight, and no one did after it was bought. The offerings for the *puja* were ready, the singers were waiting with their drums, cymbals and bells, while the Panchlight stood in the middle of it all. The villagers had never bought anything like this before. There is a saying in the village: 'Shall we buy a cow? Yes, but who will milk it?'… And so it was with this contraption of nuts and bolts… 'Who will light it?'

It was not that no one in the entire village knew how to light a Panchlight. The issue here was: 'After all the preparations, the ritual offerings and *puja,* will someone from another *toli* have be brought in to help light our Panchlight? Wouldn't it be better to let it lie around? Who can bear the insults and mockery for the rest of one's life? People from the other *toli*s will taunt us at the slightest pretext, "So, you got someone from another *toli* to light your…" No, no, it is a matter of our panchayat's pride. Don't even think of asking for help from other panchayats.'

Sadness descended on the crowd. The evening darkened. No one had lit even an oil lamp in his home… Who would want a flickering oil lamp now that the Panchlight had been bought?

But it had all come to nought! And, not a word from the chief, the secretary or the orderly! The panchayat was in serious danger of losing face. Someone said in a feeble voice: 'These technical things throw their own tantrums.'

A young man arrived with the news: 'People from the Rajput Toli are going crazy laughing at us. They are saying, "Hold your ears and do five sit-ups in front of the Panchlight and it will light up on its own."'

The panchayat members heard this report and said to themselves: 'God has given them this opportunity to laugh at us, so why wouldn't they laugh?' An old man came with the grim news that

Rudal Sah, the grocer, was saying that pumping the Panchlight can be a tricky business and needs the utmost care.

Gulri Kaki's daughter, Munri, wanted to say something. The words were itching to roll off her tongue. But how could she? She knew that Godhan knew how to light a Panchlight, but she also knew that he had been ostracised by the panchayat. Munri's mother had complained to the panchayat that Godhan would look at her daughter and sing romantic songs from the movies. The panchayat members had been itching to teach Godhan a lesson: he had come from another village and started living here without ever having given so much as a paisa to the panchayat. He couldn't care less about the panchayat members. So now when the opportunity presented itself, they fined him ten rupees, and as he did not pay up, forced the villagers to ostracise him. The ban was still in place—Godhan was not allowed to talk to anyone from the *toli* or mingle socially with them. He could not even smoke from their *hukkah*s, so how could he be called now? How could Munri take his name? On the other hand, there was the question of the entire community losing face.

Munri dropped the suggestion cleverly in her friend Kaneli's ear. Kaneli smiled, 'But Godhan is debarred!' Munri said, 'Why don't you tell the chief to send for him.'

'Godhan knows how to light a Panchlight!' Kaneli announced.

'Who? Godhan? Does he? But…'

The chief looked at the secretary and the secretary looked at the other panchayat members. They had all taken a unanimous decision to ostracise Godhan. The entire village was fed up with Godhan singing lewd songs and making sheep's eyes at the girls. But the chief said, 'Why quibble over banishment from the community when the community's honour is at stake?'

The secretary said, 'True. True.'

The other members of the panchayat spoke in one voice, 'All right. Let the ban be lifted from Godhan.'

The chief dispatched the orderly. The orderly returned and said, 'Godhan refuses to come. He says there is no telling with the panchayat members; tomorrow if something goes wrong with the nuts and bolts of the contraption, they will make me pay a fine.'

The orderly pleaded, 'Please get him to agree somehow, or else it would be impossible to show our face in this village.'

Gulri Kaki spoke up, 'Shall I go and try?'

She went towards Godhan's hut and managed to mollify him. A new light of hope lit up everyone's faces. Godhan began to quietly fill the Panchlight with oil. The chief's wife shooed off the cat circling around the offerings for the *puja*. The lead singer of the troupe began to smoothen the hairs of his flick in anticipation whisking it vigorously. Godhan asked, 'Where is the spirit? How can I light it without the spirit?'

Another spanner in the works! Everyone began to harbour serious doubts about the intelligence of the chief, the secretary and the orderly—they had set out to do things without any idea of how they were to be done! Despair gripped the crowd once again. But Godhan was a clever young man. He would light the Panchlight without spirit... 'Will someone please get a little coconut oil?' Munri ran to do his bidding. Godhan began to pump the Panchlight.

The silken mesh of the Panchlight's torch slowly began to glow with light. Godhan began to alternately blow at the torch and turn its key. A sibilant hiss emerged from the Panchlight and its light began to brighten and flare. All traces of ill will seeped out from everyone's hearts. Godhan was a very bright young man.

Soon enough, the entire *toli* was lit up in the Panchlight's luminous glow. The singers sang in a high, clear voice. The bright flare of the Panchlight shone on the smiling faces all around. Godhan had won everyone's heart. Munri looked longingly at him. Their eyes met and a message flashed between them: 'Let bygones be bygones. Forgive me!'

The chief fondly called out to Godhan. Making him sit closely by his side, he said, 'You have saved our community's honour. You will be forgiven all your trespasses. You may sing as many songs from the movies as you wish!'

Gulri Kaki said, 'You must eat dinner at my house tonight.'

Godhan looked at Munri once again. Munri coyly lowered her eyelashes.

The troupe of singers finished one song and launched into loud cries of jubilation. 'Victory to… Long Live…' Every leaf and twig on every plant and bush was trembling with happiness.

The Messenger

Hargobin was surprised: so, someone could still need a messenger in this day and age. Now that even the smallest village had a post office, who would bother sending a message through a messenger? A man can send a message all the way to Lanka if he so wishes and get news from there—all the while sitting at home. Why, then, had he been sent for?

Hargobin crossed the broken porch of the big *haveli* and entered the mansion. As always, he sniffed the air to sense the message that needed to be sent...Undoubtedly, it required the utmost secrecy. Not even the sun and the moon should come to know of it, nor the birds and the bees.

He called out a greeting to Badi Bahuriya, the elder daughter-in-law of the house.

Badi Bahuriya offered him a low stool to seat himself and, by a flicker of the eye, gestured that he sit quietly for a while. The big *haveli* is now big only in name. Where once a crowd of maids and servants of all sorts milled about, today Badi Bahuriya sat winnowing the wheat with her own hands. Once the village barber-woman had fed her entire family merely by applying henna on these hands. Gone were those days. Hargobin drew a deep breath.

It was as though the last act of the play had been played out with Bade Bhaiyya's death. The three remaining brothers began to squabble over the division of the property. The tenants began to lay claim over the lands. The three brothers left the village to live in the city. Badi Bahuriya was left behind—for where could the poor thing go? God always gives good people a hard time. Or why else would Bade Bhaiyya have died so quickly in a matter of an hour's illness? The spectacle of division had been enacted by snatching away every last ornament from Badi Bahuriya's body. Hargobin was there; he had seen with his own eyes the debasement of Draupadi. Those heartless brothers had torn into three equal parts Badi Bahuriya's expensive Banarasi saris. Poor, poor Badi Bahuriya!

The old village grocer-woman had been sitting in the courtyard for God knows how long, muttering to herself, 'It is all very well to buy on credit but when I come to ask for my money, my words sound bitter. Today I will go only after I get my money.'

Badi Bahuriya did not respond.

Hargobin drew another long breath. Badi Bahuriya wouldn't say a word till the grocer-woman sat there. He couldn't stay quiet any longer. He said to the grocer-woman, 'Have you learnt these skinflint methods of extracting your money from the Kabuli moneylenders?'

The woman heard the word 'Kabuli' and flew into a rage, 'Keep quiet, you whisker-less rascal!'

'What can I do if God didn't give me a moustache or a beard like the venerable Agha Sahab from Kabul?'

'If you say the word "Kabul" again, I will pull your tongue out.' Hargobin stuck his tongue out as though to say: 'Here, pull it.'

Five years ago, a certain Gul Mohammad Agha used come to the village and sell cloth on credit from a shack outside the grocer-woman's shop. Agha was a sweet-talker when he was selling his cloth but when it came to collecting payments, he turned into a heartless tyrant, extracting more than his money's worth from the hapless villagers. Finally, one day, some of his creditors got together and beat him up so badly that he never showed up in the village again. But, from that day on, the grocer woman became a termagant. Even the mention of Kabuli almonds was enough to make her fly into a rage. The troupe of village dancers staged a play on her plight. They mimicked a phoney Afghan accent and sang: *'If you come to my land, I will feed you almonds, pistachios and walnut, O Dear Grocer-woman...'*

The grocer-woman left the *haveli* muttering curses and obscenities, and Badi Bahuriya turned to Hargobin and said, 'Brother Hargobin, you have to take a message for me. Today itself. Will you go?'

'Where?'

'To my mother's.'

Drowning in Badi Bahuriya's tear-filled eyes, Hargobin said, 'Tell me, what is the message?'

Badi Bahuriya began to cry in great rasping sobs as she narrated her message. Hargobin's eyes too welled up. Hargobin could see the Lakshmi-like goddess, who had once ruled over the big *haveli,* break down virtually in front of his eyes. He said, 'You must steel yourself, Badi Bahuriya.'

'How much more can I steel myself? Tell my mother, I will serve my brothers and their wives. I will eat the leftovers from their children's plates and fill my belly, but I will not live here anymore, no I will not...Tell my mother that if she doesn't send for me, I will tie a pot around my neck and drown myself in the pond. How long can I survive on leaves and grass? Why should I? And for whom?'

Every pore of Hargobin's body twitched. How heartless her brothers-in-law and their wives were? In the month of *Aghan,* when the rice was being harvested, they would show up from the city—their wives and children in tow—stay for ten or fifteen days, work up a huge debt and return with mounds of freshly harvested rice and homemade *chewra.* They would show up again in the mango season, pluck the semi-ripe fruit, stuff it into sacks and go off. Not once would they bother to check on Badi Bahuriya—the beasts!

Badi Bahuriya untied a dirty crumpled five-rupee note from the end of her sari and said, 'I have not been able to put together enough to cover your expenses for the journey. Take the return fare from my mother, and I hope my brother returns with you.'

Hargobin said, 'You don't have to give me money for the journey. I will find the money.'

'But where will you find the money?'

'I shall leave by the ten o'clock train tonight.'

Badi Bahuriya sat there, holding the five-rupee note and looking at Hargobin with an expressionless gaze. Hargobin left the *haveli* but he clearly heard Badi Bahuriya say, 'I will wait for you to return.'

❦

Hargobin, the messenger—the one who carried messages back and forth! Everyone can't take on the job of carrying messages. A man is either born a messenger, or he isn't. It isn't easy to remember every single word of the message, the tone and manner in which it is spoken, and to convey it in exactly the same manner. The people in the village harbour the common misconception that an idle, good-for-nothing glutton ends up becoming a messenger. What else would you call one who has neither a boss nor an underling, who goes from village to village without charging a paisa as fee?...A women's flunkey! A woman only has to talk sweetly for him to fall under her spell and do her bidding! Would you call such a person a man? Yet, there isn't a single mother, sister or daughter-in-law in the village for whom Hargobin has not carried a message...But this is the first time he's carrying such a message!

Hargobin sat on the train and was swamped by memories of the old days and the countless messages he had carried. A half-remembered fragment of a poignant folksong echoed in his ears:

I fall at your feet, O Messenger
Take my message, O Messenger...

Every word of Badi Bahuriya's message pierced his heart like a thorn. How will I live here? There was one servant left—he too ran away yesterday. The cow, tethered to her post, whimpers with hunger all day long. For whom shall I carry on like this?

Hargobin asked the passenger sitting beside him, 'Does the post train stop at Thana Bihnpur station?'

The passenger snapped, 'All trains stop at Thana Bihnpur.'

Hargobin figured that his neighbour was the surly type, not given to making small talk with fellow travelers. So he went back to going over Badi Bahuriya's message, memorising each word...But how will he control himself while narrating it? Will he also cry at the exact moment that Badi Bahuriya had cried while giving him the message?

He reached Kathiar station and found that a great deal had changed in the past fifteen or twenty years. Now there was no need to get off the train and make enquiries. The moment the train halted, a voice announced on the loudspeaker: 'All passengers going to Thana Bihnpur, Khagadia and Barauni, please proceed to platform number three. The train is waiting at the platform.'

Hargobin was pleased. At Kathiar you could tell that we had truly made progress since we had gained freedom. In the past, he had missed his connecting trains simply because he would lose so much time in making enquiries about which train to board and from where.

He sat down in the connecting train and once again Badi Bahuriya's sad face appeared before his eyes...'Brother Hargobin, tell my mother, God has turned His eyes away from me, but I still have my mother...Why?...For whom?...How long shall I live on leaves and grass?'

Hargobin's heart grew heavy as the train approached Thana Bihnpur station. He had come here before—sometimes carrying glad tidings, sometimes with doleful ones, but he had never felt like this. His feet refused to move towards the village. Soon Badi

Bahuriya will take this path to reach her village. She will leave that village forever, never to return.

Once again, Hargobin's heart began to tremble. What will be left in the village if the goddess Lakshmi forsakes it?...How can he carry such a message? How can he say that Badi Bahuriya has been living on leaves and grass?...Whoever hears it will spit at the mention of his village! What sort of village is it where the goddess-like Badi Bahuriya has to suffer such ignominy?

Unwillingly, Hargobin reached the village. People recognised him instantly: The messenger from Jalalgadh has come! God knows what message he has brought!

'Ram-Ram, Brother! Is all well?'

'Ram-Ram, Brother! By the grace of God, all is well.'

'Have you had any rain there?'

Badi Bahuriya's elder brother didn't recognise Hargobin, but when he introduced himself, the first thing he asked was, 'How is my sister?'

'She is well by the grace of God.'

Hargobin was summoned to the women's courtyard after he had washed and freshened himself. Once again, he began to tremble. His heart began to beat furiously...This had never happened to him before...Badi Bahuriya's tear-filled eyes...Her message laced with sobs and whimpers...He greeted Badi Bahuriya's mother.

The old lady asked him, 'Tell me, son, what message have you brought?'

'All is well there.'

'Is there any message for me?'

'Huh? Message?...No, there is no message. I had come to Sirsiya village yesterday and I thought of visiting you.'

The old lady appeared to grow sad at this reply. 'So, you have not come with a message?'

'No, there is no message...though Badi Bahuriya did say that if she finds the time she might come to see you during Dushera.' The old lady didn't say a word. Hargobin continued, 'But when will she find the time? The burden of running the entire household is on her.'

The old lady said, 'I have been telling my son to go and fetch his sister to come and live with us. What is left for her there? All the land and property is gone. All three brothers-in-law have settled down in the city. They never bother to enquire after her. My daughter is there, all alone...'

'No, no. There is still enough land and property left. Whatever is there is more than enough. Though tumbled-down, it is, after all, still the big *haveli.* While it is true that she has no children, the whole village is her family. Badi Bahuriya is like the goddess Lakshmi in our village... Her brothers-in-law keep insisting that she goes away with them but how can the goddess leave her village and go to live in the city!

The old lady served him refreshments with her own hands. 'Eat a little first, son.'

As he ate he thought of Badi Bahuriya sitting in her courtyard waiting for him—hungry! ... In the evening, as he was served his dinner, it seemed as though Badi Bahuriya was sitting in front of his eyes... No one gives me a paisa's credit... Even a dog can find enough to fill its belly, but I?...Tell my mother...'

Hargobin looked at the platter of food before him—rice, lentils, three types of vegetables, ghee, papad, pickle... Badi Bahuriya must be boiling leaves and grass for her dinner.

The old lady asked, 'What's the matter, son, why aren't you eating?' 'I ate so much at tea time.'

'A young man can eat any amount of snacks and still consume a platter full of rice.'

But Hargobin didn't eat anything. He couldn't.

About the messengers it is said that they eat their fill and sleep soundly, but Hargobin is unable to sleep...What has he done? What has happened to him? Has he forgotten why he has come? Why did he lie?...No, no, in the morning he must give the correct message to the old lady. He must tell her everything, word for word: 'Your daughter is in a terrible difficulty. Send someone today and have her fetched. Or else, she will truly do something terrible. After all, why should she undergo this hardship any longer, and for whom?...Badi Bahuriya has said she will eat the leftovers from her nieces' and nephews' plates and live in a corner of this house...!'

Hargobin could not sleep that night.

Badi Bahuriya sat in front of his eyes all night long—sobbing and wiping her tears. In the morning he got up and hardened his heart and resolved to tell all. After all, he was a messenger. His job was to carry the message and convey it accurately. He went to sit beside the old lady to convey Badi Bahuriya's message. The old lady asked, 'What is it, son? Do you want to say something?'

'I must catch the next train. I have been away for several days.'

'What's the hurry? Stay here for a few days, be our guest and enjoy our hospitality.'

'No, no, you must excuse me this time. I will come with Badi Bahuriya at Dushera time. Then I will enjoy your hospitality for a good fifteen days!' The old lady complained, 'Why come if you were in such a hurry! I was thinking of sending some *dahi-chewra* for my daughter with you. I won't be able to send the *dahi*, but there is some *chewra* made of basmati rice, take that.'

As Hargobin left the courtyard with a bundle of *chewra* tucked under his arm, Badi Bahuriya's eldest brother called out, 'Do you have enough for the train fare, brother?'

Hargobin answered, 'Yes, with the grace of God, there is no shortage of anything.'

Hargobin reached the station and took stock of his money. He had only enough money to buy a ticket till Kathiar. And, if the four *anna* coin turned out to be fake, only till Saimapur. He could never even think of traveling without a ticket. The blood in his body would dry up with terror.

His condition took a turn for the worse the moment he sat down in the train. Why had he come here? And why was he returning without accomplishing his mission? What would he say to Badi Bahuriya?

If the blind beggar singing *nirguna* songs had not entered his compartment, who knows how far his condition would have deteriorated? He took heart from the words of the blind beggar's song and felt better:

The happiness of my father's home appears like a dream now
The palanquin leaves for my husband's home
Don't cry, brother, for this is my fate....

When the blind beggar left, Badi Bahuriya emerged from his heart and began to cry again—For whom should I undergo these hardships?

At five in the morning he reached Kathiar station. The loudspeaker was announcing: 'Passengers travelling to Bairgaddi, Kusiar and Jalalgadh should proceed to platform number one.'

Hargobin had to go to Jalalgadh but how could he go to platform number one. He had a ticket only till Kathiyar. And Jalalgadh was twenty *kos* away...Badi Bahuriya must be waiting for him...What was twenty *kos*, after all? He would walk.

Hargobin took the name of Lord Hanuman, the great warrior, and set off. For ten *kos* or so, he cruised along as though on a 'high'. He reached a small town and drank his fill of water. He sniffed the bundle of *chewra* under his arm—Aaah! The smell of *chewra* made from basmati rice. A mother's gift to her daughter! No, he cannot eat even a handful of this—what will he say to Badi Bahuriya?

His feet trembled...No, he wouldn't stop to think, not now. Now he must walk. He must walk quickly because he must reach his village...Badi Bahuriya's tear-drenched eyes were pulling him towards the village...I will wait for you to return.

Fifteen *kos*...Tell mother I can't take it anymore. Sixteen... seventeen... eighteen...the signal at Jalalgadh station can be spotted now...The tall palm tree in the village raises its head to watch him approach. Under that very palm tree, sitting in her courtyard inside the big *haveli*, Badi Bahuriya must be keeping a silent vigil, waiting for him with her eyes glued to the door, hungry and thirsty.

I fall at your feet, O Messenger
Take my message, O Messenger...

But what is this? Where has he reached? Which village is this? And why the dense darkness of a moonless night...A river? Where has the river come from? No, no, it isn't a river...these are fields...And is that a cluster of huts or a herd of elephants? Where did the palm go? Has he lost his way?...Not a trace of light anywhere...Whom shall he ask?...Doesn't anyone live in this village?...Why is there no light?...Is that light there or are those someone's eyes? Is he standing or moving? Is he in a train or is he on the ground?

'You have come, Brother Hargobin!' Is that Badi Bahuriya's voice, or is it the loudspeaker at Kathiyar station?

'Brother Hargobin, what is the matter with you?'

'Badi Bahuriya?'

Hargobin felt with his hand and discovered he was lying down on a bedding on the floor. He touched the faint shadow sitting in front of him and asked, 'Badi Bahuriya?'

'How do you feel now, Brother Hargobin?...Here, try another sip of this milk...Open your mouth...Aaaa...drink...Drink up!'

Hargobin came to his senses. He fell at Badi Bahuriya's feet and said, 'Forgive me, Badi Bahuriya. I could not convey your message...Don't leave this village...Don't go away...I promise you will know no more hardships. I am your son. Badi Bahuriya, you are my mother, you are the mother of the entire village. I won't sit idle...I will find work. I will do all your errands...Tell me, you won't leave the village and go away, will you? Tell me...'

Badi Bahuriya put a handful of *chewra* made from basmati rice in the warm milk and stirred it. She had been regretting her error in sending the message ever since the messenger had left.

The Estrangement

It happened exactly as he had planned. The strategy he had devised over the last two years unfolded now precisely according to plan. He returned to his village by the night train. The old moneylender got wind of it that very night. The sun was yet to rise when that old scumbag hobbled to his doorstep on his wooden clogs and began to noisily clear his phlegm-choked throat, gagging and spitting blobs of mucus.

At first he thought he was in the middle of an early-morning dream. For the last two years his early-morning dreams had unfolded exactly like this!

A wheezy tobacco-racked voice emerged from a sputum-choked throat: 'Bilas-wa-aa-aa!… Aaa-ak-thooo!'

His half-dressed wife woke up from deep slumber and began to pull her disheveled clothes together. 'It's the moneylender, isn't it?'

'So, it isn't a dream. That wretch has come himself, has he?'

He was surprised… it was happening exactly as he had thought. He had been preparing himself rigorously for just this moment over the past twenty-four months. Despite that, his heart was beating furiously. A coil of fear tingled somewhere deep inside his bones. His cheeks were flushed and his temples throbbed. It was as though he had forgotten his 'part' in the 'drama' just as the curtain was about to rise.

He saw his wife's eyes filled with fear instead of sleep. There was a question in her eyes: 'Will we have to…'

His wife's fearful face pulled him up short. He muttered under his breath, 'We'll have to do nothing… And why do you look like this? What's come over you?'

Outside, the old man had withstood the first violent bout of coughing. Now his voice rang out like steel, 'Bils-ya-aa!'

Stepping out into the courtyard, he saw his mother huddled in a corner like a bundle of rags. Out of sheer fright, she was holding her hand-held *hukkah* without taking a puff, scared that the moneylender might hear it gurgle!

He pulled on a gold-buttoned t-shirt and called out from the courtyard, 'Who's there? Who's making this infernal din?'

This piercing response astonished not only his wife and mother but also the seventy-five year-old moneylender, who was the virtual master of the entire village.

His wife went towards the door with a small lamp, but he stopped her with a curt reprimand, 'Where do you think you are off to with that lamp in your hand? Go and start a fire and heat some water.'

He stepped out of the courtyard, blowing rings of smoke from his *beedi*… No, he was damned if he was going to forget the 'part' he had memorised over two years. He said, 'Yes, what is it?'

This was enough for the moneylender to read the writing on the wall… No touching of feet, not even a word of greeting, and blowing smoke in his face too!

'You have changed a great deal, Bilsiya!'

The moneylender had hit the nail on its head.

He gave his 'prepared' answer, 'What is this Bilsiya-Bilsiya? My name is Rambilas… Rambilas Singh.'

Rambilas called out to his mother, 'Ma, bring a broom and a basket of dung.'

Inside the house, Rambilas's wife looked at her old mother-in-law… First he tells me to heat the water; now he is asking for a broom and a basket of dung!

His mother called out from the courtyard in a timid voice, 'What will you do with the broom and basket, son?'

The moneylender's eyes went round. His breathing became short and furious. Such dishonour! Fear and anger combined to create a rustling in his throat and he could feel a full-throated coughing fit about to explode inside him. The more he tried to stop himself, the more severe became the need to spit out the blobs of phlegm choking his throat. His insides felt as though they would explode...

'Your wife asks what is to be done with the hot water?'

Rambilas exploded, 'She's already started her questions and counter-questions? Why do I need the hot water? What do I want to do with the broom and basket? Tell her to come out and see for herself—the entire doorway is stinking with sputum and phlegm. And, you, sir—why don't you go and spit your gob elsewhere? Go to the field if you must spit like this!'

The moneylender tried in vain to contain the coughs that racked his body and the phlegm that erupted uncontrollably. In the process, the *gamcha* on his shoulder became soiled.

Rambilas puckered his face with acute distaste. 'Why must you go around to other people's homes with such an uncontrollable cough? Why not go to a doctor and get some treatment? Get a "photo" taken; you might have T.B.'

By now, the coughing and gagging had stolen the wind from the moneylender's sails. Rambilas had thought that the very mention of T.B. would provoke quite a predictable response from that old scumbag, such as: 'Quiet, you rascal! May you and your descendents have T.B.!'

But the moneylender abandoned the 'part' he should have performed and launched into an unscripted role. He said, 'Son, what good is medicine or doctor or *vaid* to me now? How does it matter whether I have T.B. or asthma in the twilight of my life?'

... Last year, in the drama staged during Durga Puja celebrations in the Mahendrapur *muhalla*, Jugal Mahto, the *paan* seller, had messed up his lines just like this. He was supposed to enact the role of an executioner, but forgot his lines the moment he raised his sword and launched into an impromptu performance before flinging down the sword and bawling like a baby… The moneylender wasn't crying, or was he? No, no, he was simply wiping his snot.

The moneylender understood what was going on.

Rambilas's old mother came out with a broom in one hand. She called out a greeting to the moneylender but made no attempt to put down the broom and touch his feet.

But all he said was, 'God is great! I had stopped by to tell you how pleased I am to see Bilas… Rambilas *babua* back. I can only hope and pray that Bilas… Rambilas goes back with his honour and respect intact. He has done so well for himself...!'

There the moneylender went again, not keeping to his allotted 'part'. What could Rambilas say in response to this unscripted dialogue?

'We thought you had come to collect the money we owe you. I came back last night; I'm not going to run away. Anyway, now that you have come, take your money.'

The old woman asked, 'Your wife says the water has been boiled; what is to be done with it?'

'She asks questions at every step! I asked her to boil the water to make the tea.'

The moneylender said, 'We can settle our accounts later. What's the hurry?'

As he took his leave, Rambilas still didn't touch his feet.

Rambilas began to take out tea, sugar and a teacup from his new suitcase. His wife said, 'Today the moneylender was soft as *halwa* made of the finest flour. Ask your mother how he used to show up at our door twice a month with his son and threaten to take our buffalo in lieu of the money we owed him!'

'Why didn't you say it when he was here? What did you have stuffed in your mouth then? A banana?'

Rambilas remembered how he had resolved to run away to the city and earn money when he had heard the moneylender's loose talk: 'You took my money and got married. And now you sleep with one leg over your wife's and have forgotten all about my money. Huh? If I hadn't loaned you that money you wouldn't be eating these sweet morsels everyday, would you?'

The bastard! Rambilas's ears became red when he remembered those words!

'Son, there is so much you don't know. The other day, the moneylender's son showed up asking for milk. All the milk had been sold, so what could I give him? He stuck his tongue out at me and taunted as he turned to go: "The world has turned upside down. Or else, there was a time when, in this very neighbourhood, our flunkies have milked a woman when a buffalo didn't have any milk left!"'

Rambilas scalded his tongue. He puffed at his tea and repeated, 'Why didn't you tell me when he was here? What did you have stuffed in your mouth then? A banana?'

A woman's milk? It was enough to cut his heart into two.

Rambilas said to his wife, 'There is a new bodice for you. Take it out of the suitcase and wear it; it is an English-style brassiere.'

The news spread in the village with the light of the rising sun.

Bilasiya has returned home, last night. What? Don't call him Bilasiya now. Haven't you heard… how he snubbed the moneylender first thing in the morning! He said, 'Don't call me Bilasiya, say Rambilas.' And he flung a packet of two hundred rupees at the moneylender's face. And, yes, another thing—he has a license in the pocket of his kurta. A license with a government stamp! He drives a rickshaw in Patna, after all, is it any wonder that he should have a license bearing a government stamp. And do you know? He calls his wife by her name!…'Ai Jhumki!' that is what he says.

Rambilas's wife, Jhumki, went to fetch water wearing her new red brassiere. All the women crowded around her. 'Let's see the

English-style vest.' 'The *mem* types wear it.' 'See, how it rides up and shows your belly.' 'What? This bit of fabric costs five *taka*?' 'How do you wear it? It has no buttons… how do you get it on and off?' 'Does it stay in place like this all the time?' 'He must have got you a sari too?' 'When did he come in the night?' 'Early? In the first half of the night?'

Bashful and laughing, Jhumki answered, 'I got so scared when I heard footsteps. Who could be coming at that time of the night, that too, wearing metal-heeled shoes. And my mother-in-law got so scared, she went and hid in the store room. A man changes when he goes to the city, even his voice changes. But our black buffalo recognised his voice straightaway. She started lowing and, breaking her tether, ran into the courtyard to greet him, and began to lick him lovingly from head to toe. And the moment he stepped into the house, my husband taunted us, "My Black Beauty is better than my family… better than any human being!"'

'And then? What did you give him to eat at that time of the night?'

'What shall I tell you, sister, I am so embarrassed… there wasn't a pinch of rice in the house, not even a grain of *chooda* or *bhooja*. Thankfully the curd had set by then. So, he ate the curd and taunted me again, "If it weren't for my Black Beauty, I would have had to starve all night."

'And then?'

'Did you try out your brassiere at night?'

'He must have got you rose-scented oil as well.'

'And? And what else did he taunt you about?'

'Is it only his voice that has changed in the city or has…'

Jhumki made a face and smiled. The women laughed. How they loved the sight of Jhumki's red brassiere. How well it suited Jhumki! How she looked prettier than ever in it!

In the afternoon, when Jhumki came to fetch the water, she was wearing new ear rings. She looked more radiant by the hour.

And later in the day, when it was time for the women to take their bath, a crowd gathered around Jhumki. Everyone wanted to borrow her new 'Moonlight' soap and cover their bodies with its sudsy, bubbly foam. Will Jhumki use this soap everyday? She will become fair as a *mem* or *bangalin*, won't she?

And when she went to the shop, Jhumki sported a sparkling *bindi* on her forehead. On the way she met Shivdhari standing in Deaf Aunty's lane. He saw Jhumki and a shudder ran through his body. He said, 'Life will become so difficult now... What will happen to me?'

'I don't like such jokes when I am walking about in broad daylight.'

Shivdhari thought, 'Don't like such jokes? Is that what she said as she made a face and walked away? What if she goes home and tells Rambilas? He has returned from the city with a 'Singh'[1] added to his name. Let us see how long this pretense continues. Let us see how long a man, who has got used to the good life in the city, lasts out in the village. And what about me... everything I have done, all the hard work I have put in, the money I have spent, will it all go waste?'

There was a crowd at the shop but the old woman who owned it, managed to get her message across to Jhumki, 'Watch out for your mother-in-law. She might catch him when you are not there and pour her poison in his ears. Be careful that she doesn't tell him something against you that she might have picked up from the village gossip. The old hag will turn him against you and grab all his money.'

Like a demure bride, still newly-wed by village standards, Jhumki spoke from behind her veil, 'Aunty, let people say what they want. I have faith in God above. While there are all these people around

[1] Singh would indicate a higher caste, such as Thakur. Adding a 'Singh' to one's name is a symbolic assertion of upward mobility within the rigid caste system.

us in the neighbourhood and in the whole village, if it weren't for our buffalo, what would have happened to us? Everyone knows how we have eked out a living for the past two years.'

Jhumki too knew the art of getting her message across. Everyone understood. Jhumki was saying: 'If it weren't for Shivdhari, who would have taken the buffalo for grazing?' And the night 'grazing' was not exactly free.

Jhumki went on, 'We have a patch of dusty land but just having the land is not enough. It isn't a woman's job to plough and plant. It has yielded cauliflower worth twenty rupees and onion and garlic worth ten rupees in the past two years… it didn't happen on its own. There are such freeloaders in this village… everyone knows it; it is no secret. When they want it, the milk and curd are sweet, but when it is time to pay up, the grapes become sour. A woman can't waylay people when they are going to the *haat* or the bazaar and make them cough up the money that they owe her.'

On her way back, Jhumki stopped by at Deaf Aunty's place. There she met Shivdhari, looking woebegone and idly twirling a ball of twine. Jhumki spoke sternly, 'I am very angry with you. There has been a crowd of visitors streaming in since the morning. Why did you run away after milking the buffalo? … He has asked about you at least ten times since the morning. If you don't come, how will he know how you have helped us, in how many different ways at different times? I told him as much as I could about you… What are you scared of? Let him know the truth.'

Jhumki plucked a bundle of *beedis* from the basket and kept it before him. 'Here, here is your quota of *beedi-supari* for the day. If you skulk here and hide your face, he will believe whatever he is told.'

A quiver ran through Shivdhari's body. He felt life return to his limbs. Really, he is such a thick-skulled idiot! Jhumki *Bhauji's* anger is perfectly justified.

He took in the ear rings… the red brassiere, the sparkling *bindi*, the sweet-scented body… the laughter that could steal hearts.

Shivdhari's body grew hot, as though it was on fire.

He plucked a *beedi* from the bundle lying in front of him and lit it. But something got snuffed out inside him. How she had tantalised him all these days! 'Am I running away somewhere?' she would tease.

Now he would have to see her on the sly.

Shivdhari sat and puffed away for a long time, blowing clouds of smoke from his *beedi*.

A balloon of smoke has been drifting from Rambilas's doorway all morning. Waves of laughter break out every few minutes. Rambilas has been waxing eloquent about Patna, keeping his listeners enthralled with his tales.

Two years ago, in the month of *chait*, he had slunk away in the middle of the month. He had run away from the village and from the moneylender's employ, jumping the debt he owed the moneylender.

And the next day a crowd had gathered in the courtyard and at his doorstep, as it had today. But that day his mother had been crying and telling everyone how her dear boy, Bilasiya, had lost his senses from the day he had brought home his new bride. The new daughter-in-law had driven away her son.

And Jhumki had cursed her mother-in-law from behind her veil while the buffalo had lowed piteously and continuously.

And the old moneylender's flunkey, Ramsinghasan Singh, had said, 'I know exactly what is going on. Both the women are putting on an act. Bilasiya has not run away on his own; he has connived with his wife and mother before leaving the village. But where will he run away to? One day this buffalo has to be tethered at my master's door.'

'Where is that fellow? Has he left his job and gone away?' asked Rambilas now, much to the amazement of his listeners.

'Oh-oh-oh? Don't you know?' they chorused.

In the midst of all the Patna tales, here was an opportunity to tell a homespun tale and one Ghotna wanted to be the one to tell it.

'All right, Ghotna, you tell it,' the others said.

'Brother Rambilas! Last year, the newly-married daughter-in-law of one Musammat, from the Pachiali Tola, showed exemplary courage, even greater than the bravery you have shown. You know what a lecher that fellow was. The moment a new bride put her foot in the village, he would lose his sleep. Like a tomcat, he would begin to prowl around her house, and like a cat he would skim the cream off the pitcher without anyone catching him. But Musammat's daughter-in-law squeezed all the cream out of him. She caught him in such a vice-like grip that he didn't know what hit him.'

'Eh?'

'Ask the others, they will tell you. He had to be taken to the hospital at Araria and operated upon. It has been heard that the doctor at the hospital asked him whether he had got stuck between the two stones of a grain mill. And after leaving the hospital, the wretch never showed his face around here. Ha-ha-ha…'

'That woman should be given a medal by the government. Had she been in the city, the story would have been out in the papers, along with her photo…'

'How would the photo have been printed? With her holding him tight? Would it have been life-like?'

This reminded Rambilas of his own photograph. He took out the license from his pocket and showed it around. Everyone took turns to hold the photograph-bearing rickshaw-driver's license in their hand and look at it. No, clearly, Rambilas is not lying. Some people had wrongly spread the rumour that he was washing dishes in a Christian hotel. Actually, it wasn't 'some people'; it was that Dubey's elder son who had sworn by his sacred *janeo* thread and said that he had seen Rambilas doing that with his own eyes.

Everyone fell silent as Shivdhari approached. Does Rambilas know what has been going on behind his back? He will kill Shivdhari the moment he finds out. How long can such things stay hidden?

'There you are, Shivdhariya, where have you been missing all morning?'

'I had gone till the station, brother.'

Rambilas's wife has, no doubt, thrown the water from her pot and come out on the pretext of fetching water. After all, how can she stay indoors after hearing Shivdhari's voice?

She returned with the water and spoke from behind her veil, 'Sehjo Aunty was asking why our house smells like the houses in the Muslim quarter? Is a hen's egg being cooked or what, she wanted to know?'

God knows what got into Rambilas. He said, 'A hen will be cooked here tomorrow. I will see who will stop me… What a place! I had a pinch of *garam masala* put in my potatoes and the smell of a hen's egg has spread all over the village!'

Shivdhari said, 'This village is matchless. You will find lots of people here who can make a wingless bird fly.'

'In the city a man calls his wife by her name. Why should it matter to anyone if I call my wife by a thousand different names?'

And Rambilas called out to his wife, 'Ai Jhumki! Shivdhariya has come. Send a *kulfi* for him.'

In the house, the daughter-in-law said to her mother-in-law, 'Mai, have you heard what he's saying?'

The old woman was pleased by the son who had earned big bucks, just as she was by the smell of the *masalas* in the kitchen. 'What is there to listen to? A man will talk and behave as others do where he lives.'

'I will drink tea all day long and alcohol all night long if I please… How does it matter to others? Shivdhariya, is the alcohol sold at the railway station any good, or is it mixed with water? I am going to down two bottles today.'

What would poor Shivdhariya know about alcohol; he can tell you about *ganja*.

'Ai Jhumki! Why do you wear such a long veil?'

Embarrassed, Jhumki ran towards the courtyard.

Everything was happening as planned. All the dreams Rambilas had dreamt in distant Patna were coming true. He had succeeded in pulling out the poisonous fang of the moneylender and flinging it away. The entire village was going hurrah over his victory. In every home in the village his name was being taken at least ten times a day. What a son! What a husband! Everyone agreed.

His door front has become like the porch of the moneylender who is the virtual owner of the village. Even the young men from the Brahmin and Rajput *tola*s come and sit with him. All day long, there are rounds of tea, *beedi*s and cards, and, at night, English-style 'cards'.

The moneylender's elder son had sat playing cards with Rambilas all day. As evening fell, Rambilas said, 'Now we will play cards in the English style? Will you stay? For just one sip?'

Now the moneylender's son comes every evening, drinks an ounce but pays for one whole bottle.

All the young men in the village want to go to Patna with Rambilas this time. After all, who would want to stay in the village after listening to Rambilas's lip-smacking city-slicker tales?

'Rajinder Nagar? Now, how do I tell you what it's like? It is as though the government engineer went to Lord Indra's city, took a photo and came back and built a city exactly like it. Colorful flowers on either side of the road and sitting in the middle of every flower-bearing bush, is a girl singing a song!'

'Eh! Then, truly, it must be like Lord Indra's paradise!'

'I tell you, when you see the *jamadarin*[2] of Patna—and by *jamadarin* I don't mean the policeman's wife but the woman who

[2] *Jamadar* was the village policeman, so the *jamadarin* was understood to be his wife in the village; but *jamadarin* is also used for a woman, usually from the lower castes, who cleans for a living.

sweeps the streets—you will mistake her for some big zamindar's wife.'

'You mean she is so beautiful?'

'So what if she is dark-skinned? The real thing is her body, the way she is built. There is one called Rajbatiya. She lives near our rickshaw stand. The wretch sets out every morning wearing a printed sari, carrying her broom on her shoulder, as though she is going out to conquer some kingdom… not sweep the road!'

'Eh!'

Why would any young man want to stay on in this miserable village?

Brother Rambilas, I will also go with you this time. And me! And me, too! Here, we plough the fields all the year round for a miserable 108 rupees. And there you can earn 200 rupees in one month! Rambilas Kaka, take me along! Don't forget me, Rambilas! If not driving a rickshaw, get me a job in a hotel. I will take up any job. That day you were telling us how scrap-dealers do a roaring business selling old newspapers and glass bottles.

Except Shivdhari, everyone else has decided to go to the city. In fact, Shivdhari has never so much as mentioned the subject of going to the city.

Everything has happened as planned but, every few days, time and again, a small thorn suddenly gets embedded in Rambilas's mind like a stabbing dagger. That night why did Jhumki say that? Why? 'Everything is all right, except…'

'Except what? Tell me.'

Jhumki had simply closed her eyes and smiled.

'Why have you closed your eyes?' he had asked.

'Why do you still have the lantern on? Snuff it out…'

Unwillingly, Rambilas had lowered the wick in the lantern, but Jhumki had insisted, 'No, put it out.'

The wretch… is she a woman or a bat?

Shivdhari smokes *ganja*; despite everyone's insistence he has so far not taken even a sip of alcohol. Not even a drop to taste.

In the morning, as soon as Rambilas woke up, that night's incident drove into his heart like a piercing dagger. 'Everything is all right, except…'

There are only four days left now. A song of separation hums in Rambilas's ears at all hours… poignant, sorrowful words echo around him.

All the young men in the village who have decided to go with Rambilas have had their haircut at the market near the railway station. Rambilas had told them that in the city people can tell, at one glance, where you have come from, by the way your hair has been cut. Every fibre in their bodies is tingling with excitement at the prospect of leaving the village, but, every now and again, a thorn pierces Rambilas's heart.

Tonight he shall ask Jhumki once again.

'There are only four days left to go.'

'Uh, ummm.'

Rambilas stayed quiet. After a long silence, his wife asked, 'When will you come again?'

'Who knows?'

He hasn't been drinking tonight. The liquor sold at the station market is undiluted, like the village milk. One sip is enough to make the heady brew go straight to one's head. Tonight he has told everyone… there shall be no English-style 'cards' tonight.

Jhumki did not respond to Rambilas' cryptic answer. But she is awake; he knows that.

'Jhumki.'

'Hunnn… Why haven't you been drinking tonight?'

'I shall stay awake all night.'

And he really did stay awake all night, and, at the break of dawn, when the crows and koels began to speak to each other, Jhumki said, 'Lower your tone; speak softly…'

Now there are only three days left. On the fourth day, scores of young men shall leave the village by the Baroni Passenger train—almost everyone except Shivdhari. In fact, Shivdhari hasn't been coming to milk the buffalo for the past couple of days; Rambilas has been doing that himself.

'Jhumki?'

'Yes, what is it?'

'Tonight I have smoked *ganja* instead of alcohol. I feel as if I am flying!'

'Shivdhari won't be coming to graze the buffalo at night; his deaf aunt came to say so.'

'Let the bugger go to hell; I'll arrange for a grazer from tomorrow.'

'Where will you find a grazer for your buffalo?'

'Why?'

'You are running off with all the young men from all the peasants' and grazers' families.'

'Who said I am running off with them?'

'Every householder in the village is saying that.'

'Not every householder… only that Shivdhariya of yours must be saying it.'

Jhumki stayed silent. Rambilas prodded her with his knee and said, 'I am right, am I not?'

'Whatever you say.'

'I am right, am I not?'

Jhumki drew a long breath.

'I am right, am I not?'

'Hunnn…'

'You can have all the fun you want after four days.'

'How does it matter to you whether I have fun or die…? The sweeper Rajbatiya will have fun with you.'

'What did you say?'

Jhumki stayed silent. Rambilas prodded her with his knee once again and demanded, 'What did you say?'

'Kill me... if that is what you want to do.'

'You wretch... I will kill you and your Shivdhariya before I go.'

There was murder in his eyes. Tonight he had smoked two pots of *ganja*.

'Don't shout.'

'You wretch... the biggest barristers of Patna could not silence my tongue and you say don't shout!'

'Fine... keep shouting.'

'I haven't drunk liquor tonight. Why have you turned your back on me? Turn around, look at me, you...'

'No.'

'B-b-b-bitch!'

Rambilas will surely kill her tonight. He will tear her limb from limb... 'What do you think of me?... Eh?... Does a man become a eunuch if he drives a rickshaw?... Eh?... Tell me... You say they are all lies... Was it that Shivdhariya who took a loan from the moneylender, on four times the interest, to marry you?... Eh?... Tell me... you bitch... Swear... What do you take me for?... Do you think, by living in the city, by drinking liquor, a man... You bitch... I understand everything...'

Jhumki kept crying for a long time. When Rambilas was preparing to leave the bed, she caught hold of his vest.

'What is it?' he said.

'Don't go to Patna.'

'What's this rubbish?'

'No, really, I beg you, don't go.'

'Hunh... how will we manage if I don't go to the city?'

'How do all the others manage?'

'Unnh.'

'All right, then, take me along.'

'And Shivdhariya?'

Jhumki burst into tears. The sun had risen as high as a bamboo staff. The old mother-in-law was calling out, '*Bahu-u-u.*'

The village youth fell from the skies in unison. Today Rambilas was heard telling the crowd who usually collected at the moneylender's 'durbar' that he was happy with the half roti he ate at his own home. After all, what's so special about the city? You spend four times what you earn in the blood you burn. There is no comparison with the village... After all, the moneylender did not take a paisa extra as interest on the remaining amount. Would anyone let the interest go in the city... Be it Patna or Delhi, there is no comparison with the joys of the village... not even the kingdom of Lord Indra can match it!

... It's being said that the moneylender's son will set up a flour grinding mill. And Rambilas will be its manager.

... It's being said that all the householders in the village have collectively bribed Rambilas. After all, their sons, who constituted the entire village's population of peasants and grazers, were planning to run away with him.

... It's being said that Rambilas had got entangled with a female sweeper in the city, and that is why he doesn't want to go back. The sweeper is carrying his baby.

And, on the fourth day, everyone heard that Shivdhari had left the village and run away. He had been seen dead drunk at the station market the day before.

His deaf aunt was heard telling people that Rambilas's wife had come at dusk and had a long hush-hush conversation with him. And in the night Shivdhari had disappeared into thin air.

Rambilas said to his wife, 'Jhumki, it's being said that the Shivdhariya fellow has run away.'

'He has run away with my twenty rupees.'

'Why didn't you tell me sooner? Did you have a banana stuffed in your mouth?'

'Who could have known that he would turn out to be so dishonest?'

'You are not a good judge of character.'

'Well, the swine will show up one day, sooner or later... I will ask him then!'

Rambilas pulled Jhumki towards himself and clutched her to his chest. With his arms around her in a tight embrace, he said, 'Let the fellow go to hell! He will never be able to return from the city. The liquor will eat him alive... You wait and see!'

Jhumki got up with a start, 'Why is the buffalo keening like that?'

Rambilas answered, 'I will have to look for a male for her first thing tomorrow morning. It looks like she is in "heat".'

Jhumki blushed like a newly wed bride and smiled. And Rambilas got high without drinking even a drop of liquor.

'Ei... do you want to taste the liquor? Just a tiny sip?'

Jhumki began to laugh, 'No! No! No! Yuck... The smell of liquor makes me... Ughh!'

Old Story, New Moral

A depression in the Bay of Bengal causes a cyclone to rise.

The snow on some Himalayan peak melts. Rain-heavy clouds begin to gather and unleash their fury over the dense jungles of the Terai. The plains await the impending catastrophe, tense and still.

The cattle grazing beside the banks of the Kari-Kosi river sniff something in the air and shy away in startled panic. An old cow runs helter-skelter with her tail in the air. The old cowherd looks closely at the water in the river. He cups a handful; it is cold and sweet. He sniffs it. It smells of the earth and is reddish-ochre.

Reddish water means water from the hills—does it mean floodwaters are soon to be upon them?

The young cowherd scoffs at his words and laughs at his fears. But the shivering increases in the bodies of the animals. They stand in a herd beside the riverbank, staring at the swirling waters and showing increasing signs of panic. And not one of them—not even the newest-born calf—puts his mouth to the grass to graze.

Fields of tender wheat, corn and jute spread out on either side of the tributaries of the Kari-Kosi—the Pariar, Bakra, Lohandra and Mahanadi rivers—as though someone has painted the land a rich, dark green with a coarse thick brush. Mango groves and courtyards in village after village echo with the sweet songs of

Madhushravani. And in the air there is the heady smell of the red, fuschia and yellow veils belonging to the brides, fluttering and drying in the breeze. And a sweet sinfulness awakens in the heart of the middle-aged peasant lying atop the rough platform to keep watch over his tender milky corn, as his eyes fall on the group of robust dark young Musahari women busy cutting the wild spinach growing among the crop. He begins to sing songs of *viraha* in a loud and lusty voice:

'Beat the old ape! Look at him, lusting after pomegranates in his old age!' says one of the women.

And the rest break out in a fit of giggles, falling over each other.

Within seconds the dark giggling Musahari girls disappear into the evening gloom, as do the jute fields. And the sun that had guarded over them too sinks below the horizon. Darkness descends.

A drizzle starts. An intoxicating, unchecked joy kept hidden inside the heart all the year round, takes the form of a monsoon raga and emerges in full-throated abandon: 'It was love that made Lord Rama build a bridge across the waters...'

The easterly wind sings and dances and whirls inside a bamboo grove. And keeping tune with it, countless spirits and demonesses swing from the branches of the trees, chuckling and whooping with fearsome delight.

In the patter of the rain a piteous indistinct cry emerges from the darkness to shivers through the village: 'He-e-e-e-o-o-o-o-o!'

Is it a woman who has lost her way, calling out for help in the darkness?

The spirits of the bamboo grove run towards the fields with countless flickering fireflies studded in their veils... Mothers clutch scared children to their bosom. Someone standing in a field far away beside the river bank again cries out for help. 'He-e-e-e-o-o-o-o-o!'

Why is the goddess of the fields crying in the middle of the night?

Is disaster about to strike?

The cry for help grows faint and, in its place, there is a roar, a terrifying thunderous angry growl: 'Gooo-o-o-o...'

Is it the roar of an aeroplane overhead?

The growl seems to be coming closer. The people from the northern-most villages shout in one voice—a shout that emerges from countless terrified throats: 'Floods! O God, help!'

'Floods?'

'The waters of the Bakra river are sloshing past its eastern and western banks. There is water up till the waist beside the boundary of my fields.'

'Have pity on us, Queen Kosi!'

The people of this area call every big and small stream Kosi... Can there be floods even after the Kosi Barrage has been built upstream? ... Can man win against Mother Kosi? ... See what happens when you try to dam the Kosi!

'What will happen now?'

A bolt of thunder crackled and lightning struck one of the fields. The light in the eyes of the villagers dimmed... The world is drowning in a liquid darkness... It is the end of the world... Disaster! Catastrophe!

Hapless villagers try to pacify Mother Kosi by beating their drums and cymbals and singing songs of appeasement.

Young men from the villages set about cutting lathes and bamboo to construct makeshift shelters.

Shrill voices emerge from fearful throats to the accompaniment of drums and cymbals: 'O Mother Kosi, I fall at your feet! I will offer flowers to you-o-o-u-u-u...'

The only literate madman from the northern-most village goes about reciting verses of the poet Nagarjun, to the accompaniment of the drums, saying over and over again: *'Ta-ta-thaiya, ta-ta-thaiya, dance, dance, Kosi Maiya!'*

And dancing to the tune of these words, Kosi Maiya indeed comes traipsing into the village and, in the blink of an eye, fields and granaries, homes and barns and trees, everything begins to dance to this tune: *Ta-ta-thaiya, ta-ta-thaiya, Dhin-tak-dhinna, Chhamak-kat-chham!*

Her mouth gaping wide, riding atop a gigantic crocodile, the ten-armed Kosi sweeps heedlessly on, laughing and playful, surging on and on.

Now there are no drums and cymbals, no songs and pleas—only clamour and confusion!

Yet the youth are steadfastly at work, putting up raised platforms and shelters above the swirling waters, slashing banana plants to make enclosures... As long as one's breath doesn't stop, there is hope!

'The water has reached the verandah!'

'The calf is being swept away! Hold it! Catch it!'

'Whose house has fallen?'

'The water is swirling about the waist!'

'Who is that climbing the palm?'

'The water has entered the house! Father! Help!'

'Climb onto the thatch!'

'Mother! Help! I'm gone! ... Father! Help! ... Watch it! ... Be careful! ... There, there... Hey Sugni! ... Ramlalva! ... O Dear Lord Mahadev! ... I am drowning! Help! ... The water has reached the chest in the courtyard! ... Not here, not here! This thatch is not strong enough! ... Snake! Snake! ... Where is the rope? ... Here, pass the sickle... *Ta-ta-thaiya, ta-ta-thaiya, Dance, Dance, Kosi Maiya, Dhin-tak-dhinna, Chhamak-kat-chham!*'

In the patchy light of early morning, the old vulture sitting on the plume of the tallest palm in the village sees that for miles all round there is nothing but swirling, lapping ochre waters, and in the middle, occasional islands of what were once villages, and in these villages, one or two houses, and sitting on their roofs, a huddle of people. And there, in the distance, the corpse of a buffalo, and beyond that, drowned fields showing the drooping plumes of wilted maize.

The vulture spreads its wings and takes off!

A gaggle of wild geese search for their nests and eggs. The lapwing sings its doleful song of doom and disaster.

The clouds gather once again. The wind picks up once more. Mercy! Have mercy on us!

❦

The dream of this area's lifelong Servant of the People—the candidate defeated in the last elections—has finally come true! Mother Kosi has, at long last, given him yet another opportunity to 'serve' the people. Glory to thee, Mother! May you live long! This time, God willing, he will not rest until he defeats his opponent. He is busy trying to establish telephonic contact with the District Magistrate and various Ministers of State from the office of a merchant in Ramnagar: 'Hello! Hello!'

The regional correspondent of a major Delhi-based newspaper has come across a major breaking news after years, but: 'What? You don't have telegram forms? … Trrrrinnngggg.'

'Hello! Hello! Hello Purnea, Hello Patna, Hello Kathiar! … Trrrrinnngggg.'

'Hello, I am the party leader Sharma speaking. About fifty villages are completely drowned. No, sir, not boats, villages… villages are drowned. I can't hear you… Sir, the DM must be informed, sir… What, sir? … The MLA? … But, sir, he is from the opposition party! … Sir? Sir? … Hello? Hello?'

The party worker caught hold of the newspaper reporter at the post office counter and took him to a tea stall to give his account. But the tea stall was not the best place for such a narration. So he took him to his camp and said, 'Write… let it be remembered that such a flood has never struck before…'

'But ten years ago…'

'Who remembers what happened ten years ago? Now, write, as soon as I got the news, I reached the flood-affected areas in the middle of the night... Make sure my statement goes off today. Mine should be the very first response in print.'

The reporter makes use of his journalistic horse sense: 'But the MLA has already given his statement—to the First Press of India—on the telephone itself.'

Sharma's face fell... God has granted him this opportunity to serve the people after so long and the opponent gets the first shot at making a statement to the press? The enemy gets to be first? At the time of the Chinese invasion too, he had got left behind in making speeches and collecting funds. And this time, again?

'Look here, how many flood-affected villages did I say? Fifty? Make it two hundred and fifty... If more villages are affected, we will get more "relief" for this district. I can do anything for the good of my people and my district. And if it so pleases God, by tomorrow two hundred villages can get submerged.'

After giving his statement to the reporter, he called an 'urgent and critical' meeting of his party workers. The issue he had failed to mention in his statement came in for close scrutiny at this meeting: 'The *kasbah* of Rampur is under threat this year because of the dam built at Bardaha last year. If there is nowhere for the water to go, it might just push its way till the wagoneers' neighbourhood by the morning.'

The brave workers who live in the wagoneer's neighbourhood look at each other. A silent signal passes among them and a resolution is passed to engage in some secret activities.

Early next morning the reporter sent another urgent despatch: 'Last night another two hundred and fifty villages got submerged due to the breaking of the Bardaha Dam.' And Sharma was working the telephone lines again: 'Hello! Hello! Hello Patna, Hello Patna...'

The traders and moneylenders of Rampur *kasbah* were quick to understand that such an opportunity for 'auspicious gain' did not come by everyday. At the time of the Chinese invasion they had missed the bus. This time, while all the fuss was going on about the drought, God had sent them the floods. Who would not wash his hands in the river Ganges if it flows past their door! Their godowns and granaries are emptied overnight. Their books and ledgers become perfect and accounted for. They give generously in response to every government and non-government appeal to donate for the flood-stricken. But wheat? Where was the wheat?

The government servants clamped government locks and seals on their empty godowns.

'Brothers! Brothers! This evening… there will be… a grand assembly… of the people of Rampur… at the local town hall… that is… the Theatre Hall… to set up a committee… for the flood-affected. Brothers! Brothers! …'

'Dear Brothers! Tonight there will be a great family drama on the silver screen of the Ansari Touring Cinema… Dear Brothers! Tonight…'

'If you don't have eyes, you have nothing! Those brothers who suffer from redness in the eyes, or watering eyes, or those who have cataract and night blindness, must try our company's famous and renowned ointment…'

'What shall I do, dear Lord, I am stuck with an old man…'

'It's in the papers! It's in the papers! The latest news about this district! Two hundred villages are drowned!'

'It's here! It's here! The cheapest cloth from Bombay! …'

'It's come! It's come! The relief wagon has come! …'

'It's come! It's coming! Three dozen boats are coming! …'

'The Minster for Irrigation is coming!'

'Donate generously, Brother, give rice-clothes-money…'

'Long live Freedom!'

The boys of the two schools of Rampur *kasbah*—the Middle and the Higher Secondary—take out processions, singing songs and collecting old clothes. By evening they have split into two groups. The quarrel flares from arguments to abuses, and knives and bamboos are taken out to beat each other. All day long the boys from the Middle School shouted slogans and sang songs, but when it came to putting down the leaders' names for the records, the boys from the Higher Secondary School walked away with all the credit. Beat them up, the rascals!

The Servant of the People, Sharmaji is elected undisputed to the post of Chairman of the Relief Committee. The MLA came in for a lot of drubbing from the people: 'You were going on and on when you had come to ask for our votes; now, forget about relief supplies from the government, you haven't been able to get us even a single broken-down boat? ... Come on, answer us... how did this flood happen? ... If no one listens to you, you must resign.'

The MLA's 'militant workers' were absent, or else things would have begun with stone-throwing and gone on to...

All the famous leaders of the major political parties have descended on Rampur *kasbah* with their entourage of 'workers'. Each has set up his own camp.

A group of government doctors and nurses has just arrived. Government officers are occupying every room in the Dak Bungalows. A Coordination Meeting has been convened.

Each political party has proposed a representative's name for membership to the Vigilance Committee. Almost every party is split into two groups: the 'official' group and the 'dissident' group. In every camp a half-buried discontent smoulders.

'... Tomorrow the Chief Minister will make a "flying inspection".'

'... The Union Minister for Food and Civil Supplies is also flying down.'

'... The Minister for River Valley Development has issued a statement.'

'... And the relief is on its way. Ten trucks laden with rice-flour-oil-cloth-kerosene-matches-sago are on their way.'

'... Yesterday the Vigilance Committee meeting lasted all night.'

'Brothers! This evening... there will be a public gathering... on the Municipal Grounds... where the strictest discontent will be expressed... against the present government's relief efforts... and the arbitrary setting up of the Relief Committee.'

'Brothers! Come! Tomorrow at 10.30 am… to launch… a fast unto death… in front of… Comrade Choube… the Resident Relief Officer…'

'… Go, go, go away, you rogue. You have no faith. No faith and no shame. Go, go, go away, you rogue…'

'Brothers! …'

❦

Helpless, starving and thirsty people surrounded by water on all sides—marooned atop thatches, trees and mounds—saw the boats arrive.

The nearest boat has a flag—a Congress flag!

The one behind has one too, but it is a different colour!

'… Long live Mahatma Gandhi!'

'Huh? Why Mahatma Gandhi? What has he got to do with anything?'

'Don't get so excited, or the branch will break.'

'A third boat! No, it isn't a boat. It's the corpse of a cow with two vultures sitting astride it.'

'Aeroplane! Aeroplane!'

The boats draw closer. The Servant of the People himself rides the first one. A 'mike' is fitted on his boat. He has been laying the groundwork, as it were, from far off: 'Brothers, even though you did not vote for me in the last election, I contacted the Chief Minister, the Food Supplies Minister and the Irrigation Minister as soon as I heard of your plight…'

The workers of the opposition party ride the second boat. In one voice, they oppose Sharmaji's claims: 'This is most unfair! You are using the government boat and government aid to wrongfully campaign for the party…'

Sharmaji is the Chairman of the Relief Committee. He is unmindful of the opposition. He carries on: 'Brothers, you must give your names to our workers, down to every last man. Do not clamber onto the boats all at once. Brothers, we have as yet little staff. The boats too are few. So you must distribute whatever little there is, peacefully and amicably among yourselves…'

The boat carrying the Chairman of the Relief Committee sprinkles the submerged villages with speeches and goes away. The people in the boat directly behind it oppose every word. A few workers step off the boats, carrying ledgers and account books.

'A bigger boat is on its way.'

'Brother, is there only a boat coming or does it carry something? The children are faint with hunger. My daughter is about to die…'

Two dozen boats plied the waters till the evening, gathering people. At night thc relief officer told the Vigilance Committee in plain words: 'The boats must not carry the flag of any political party… Nothing should be given without taking a thumbprint or signature… We simply can not provide *bidi*s… It is unethical to either praise or criticise any political party while distributing relief supplies. Those who continue to indulge in such practices will henceforth not be given any responsibilities by the committee.'

There is no work yet for the doctors and nurses. They are busy playing 'indoor' and 'outdoor' games—'Game-ball' … 'Two spade' … 'Hey Miss Bannerji' … 'No trump'.

Arrangements have been made for the flood-affected villagers on the high ground near the railway bridge—under the trees, beside the *haat,* in the school compound. Arrangements have been made for people to stay in villages where the floodwaters have not entered but which are surrounded by the high waters. Boats ply the waters regularly, carrying rations to and fro. Several groups of doctors and nurses have been deployed to run health centres at such places.

The waters are gradually receding.

The Musahar and ferrymen are beginning to feel cooped up in the camps. These free-spirited people hear the news of the receding waters and become restless. They are creatures of the water. They can stay for months in mud and water… Their thumbs have blackened with all the thumb imprints they have been giving… It is far better to beg for a living than to touch the *halwa-puri* provided as relief. 'No, no… That dog-faced officer was trying to entice my Sugni, did you know? … A bunch of thieves, that's what they are!'

'Brothers! Before you leave the camp… you must… inform your "in-charge". People can return… to those villages… where the water has receded. Twine-Bamboo-Poles… and other essentials… shall be provided… for your relief and rehabilitation…'

'Brothers! It is important that you know… that gross misappropriation… of funds… has taken place… in the supplies directed towards your relief. You must… raise your voice… against the existing committee…'

'Brothers! Brothers! Hear! Hear! Friends!'

With cries of 'Brothers! Brothers!' the announcers belonging to the two opposing parties begin by calling each other liars and thieves, and end up in fisticuffs. The police resort to 'lathi-charge' to maintain peace and harmony. Several flood-affected people end up spending the night in police custody.

A major newspaper from Delhi publishes an expose: 'The engineers of the Public Works Department have shown remarkable short-sightedness in building several small dams on minor rivers and their tributaries, such as the old distributaries of the Kosi. That is why those villages, which were never affected by the floods, are submerged this year. Inept government servants…'

Another daily newspaper places the blame squarely on the officials of a neighbouring country: 'In building a barrage close to the border of our state, the neighbouring kingdom has stopped the drainage outflow of all the small rivers in northern Bihar. A flood such as this would never have happened had the concerned officials bothered to consult our experts before building the barrage.'

The local newsweekly, or shall we say the district rag, declares this flood a 'man-made' calamity and announces: 'It isn't the neighbouring state, but the oarsmen of the neighbouring country who have drowned us!'

Eventually, rats are found to be responsible for the breaking of the Bardaha Dam. They had dug up countless tunnels through its foundation, making it weak and porous in less than a year!

'... Read! Read! ... The latest news! There is a state-wide agitation! Preparations are underway... for a No-Confidence Motion... against the present government! A fast-unto-death... at the Chief Minister's residence!'

A relief boat carrying fifty tins of kerosene and ten sacks of flour and rice is said to be lost in the waters of the Panar rivulet... Drowned!

The opponents of Sharmaji have filed a suit against him. Let them! Sharmaji's task is accomplished. The district echoes with the praises showered on him. All the heartache of losses incurred during the Chinese invasion and the defeat in the last election are gone. He has reaped the benefits several times over... Surely there is a God somewhere... There is justice.

... Brothers!

... *O my countrymen, let the tears seep into your eyes...*

*

A flock of vultures soars in the skies—countless dark wings, like black clouds hovering overhead.

And on the earth bloated carcasses of dead animals. And destroyed crops and rotting plants in the fields.

The stink! Oh, that terrible odour!

Mud everywhere, and wriggling earthworms, and crawling insects, on the rotting corpse of the earth.

Straggling groups of people—heads bent, clutching babies, herding their pitifully few cocks, hens, goat and sheep, some on wagons and carts, others on their shoulders—are returning to villages, where neither a trace of their huts remains nor even a pinch of grain in their fields. But their feet are racing homeward. After nearly 30–35 days of hellish exile, a flood of love has overwhelmed their hearts—love for their homeless villages and muddy fields... For miles on end, their footprints are embossed on the mud.

The villages are coming alive once again.

The gods have come once again to live in these spirits buried under government relief, debt and assistance. For the past 30–35 days they have quarreled and fought amongst each other for life, for survival, and have begged and pleaded with government officials for relief supplies. Greed made them fight, steal, covet... Satan had come home to roost in their hearts.

In the month of *Ashwin* the sun appears without fail, to awaken the earth. Green tufts of grass glimmer in the drying mud.

A skein of wild geese circles above, crying 'paink-paink'. At this moment everything seems dear and sweet—even the kites, crows and vultures. Are those cranes in the water-filled ditches or *Koka* flowers? Branches of the *Haarsinghar* are heavy with sweet-smelling flowers. The lilt of welcome, of new arrival, is in the air. The mother is coming! That beggar woman? Is she the Goddess Annapurna, the provider, the fertile Mother Goddess?

Blowing a life-giving chant into the idol of mud and clay, the child of the soil cries: 'Mother! Forgive us!'

Everywhere there is the beating of drums to mark the beginning of prayers.

The *Ashtami* moon laughs amid the clear serene waters of the Kari-Kosi. A fragment of a song sung by the refugee boatmen from Bengal breaks and wafts away, like the delicate blossoms of *Rajnigandha* flowers: 'O my brotherrrr! ... O-o-o-o...'

The only literate madman in the district is going around reciting this one line from the poet Nirala: 'A lump of soil has become a sugar-coated sweet.'

The Queen of Hearts

'Hey, Birju's mother, won't you go to see the dance?'

Birju's mother was sitting in her courtyard, peeling sweet potatoes and simmering with quiet rage. Her seven-year-old son, Birju, had just been smacked several times and was now rolling in the dirt, getting himself thoroughly dirty. And that wretched girl, Champiya—there was no trace of her! She had been sent to the grocer to buy some *gur* when the sun had been only halfway across the courtyard; it was nearly time to light the lamps and she still hadn't returned. Let her come!

The poor billy goat was riddled with ticks, and so it was kicking its feet and running about. Birju's mother had already found an excuse to vent some of her pent-up rage on the goat. The green chilly bush that grew in the backyard... Who could have chewed it up except that miserable goat! She had picked up a clod of earth to hit it with, when that interfering old busy body, Makhni Phua, called out, 'Hey, Birju's mother, won't you go to see the dance show?'

'Birju's mother could have gone if she didn't have a nose ring in front and a tether at the back!'[1]

[1] A reference to the rope running through the nose and the tether or tail rope of a bullock's harness, it implies the various responsibilities that tie down a householder, such as those towards her husband and children.

The jabbing words dunked in hot rage pierced Phua's body. Birju's mother dropped the clod of earth, muttering, 'Ooooh, the goat is troubled enough by the ticks. Aaahhhh! Hrrrrrrr!'

Lying in the dusty courtyard, Birju lashed out at the goat with his stick. His mother felt like charging across and walloping Birju with the same stick, but the sound of laughter coming from the well near the neem tree stopped her. She merely said, 'I'll fix you good and proper! Your father has spoilt you rotten; you have become very easy with that stick of yours. Wait till I give you a taste of it!'

Makhni Phua was standing near the neem tree, bent at the waist, busily spreading the word about the ill humour and sharp tongue of Birju's mother as she rested her water pitcher and talked with the other women returning from the village well. She kept saying, as though asking for justice, 'Just look at that Birju's mother! The money from four *mann* of jute has gone to her head. You tell me... am I wrong? For the past eight days she has been going around the village telling everyone, "Birju's father has said he will take us to Balrampur by bullock-cart to see the dance. Now that we have our own bullocks, we can find a thousand carts on loan." And so I asked her just now. All the other women who are going to see the dance are finishing off their chores in a hurry to get ready. May my mouth catch fire if I meant to tease her! Do you know what she shot back at me?'

Makhni Phua twisted her lips and spoke in a mincing sort of way, 'Aaahhhh! Hrrrrrrr! ... Birju's mother could have gone if she didn't have a nose ring in front and a tether at the back!'

Jangi's daughter-in-law is not scared of Birju's mother. She spoke loudly and clearly, 'Phua, if you too had gone wearing a floral printed sari and made an offering to the officer of the Survey Settlement, you would also have been allotted two or three *bigha* of fertile land! Then your house too would have been filled with ten *mann* of golden flax harvest! You too would have bought a pair of bullocks. And then you too would have a nose ring in front and a tether at the back!'

Jangi's daughter-in-law is brash and outspoken. She is a girl who has grown up in the settlement close to the railway station. It has been barely three months since she arrived in the village as a newly wed bride and she has already picked a quarrel or two with every cantankerous mother-in-law in the Kurmi Tola.[2] Her father-in-law, Jangi, is a known criminal—a bad character registered by the police under the 'C' class. Her husband, Rangi, is well known as a stick-wielding tough guy in the Kurmi Tola. That is why she goes around looking for fights, like a ram itching to dig its horns into something.

Jangi's daughter-in-law's words, loud and defiant, reached Birju's mother like a volley of colour-filled pellets thrown during Holi, the festival of colours. Birju's mother thought of a sharp retort but refrained from venting it. Why cast a stone in a puddle of muck!

Swallowing the hot words singeing the tip of her tongue, Birju's mother once again called out to Champiya, 'O Champiya-a-a-a, I am waiting for you to come, so I can wring your neck and stuff it in the fire! ... She is becoming wayward... And all because of the theatre-bioscope-watching daughters-in-law coming to our village! Must be sitting somewhere and learning how to sing "*And the flute plays no more...*" ... O Champiya-a-a-a!'

Jangi's daughter-in-law took in the full taste and bite of these words. Balancing the water-filled pot on her waist, she twirled her hips and flounced off saying, 'Come, sister, come, let's go. The Queen of Hearts lives here. Don't you see, the electric light burns brightly in her house day in and day out, and all night long too?'

God knows why all the women present at the well laughed uproariously at the mention of the electric light. A sweet reprimand

[2] The homes in the village are segregated along caste and religious lines; such a caste- or community-specific locality is called a *tola* or *toli*. Kurmis form the largest caste group of cultivators.

lisped out from between the rows of broken teeth in Phua's mouth: 'You are the Devil's grandmother!'

Birju's mother was stunned; she felt as though someone had suddenly shone a brightly lit torch directly into her eyes... The mention of the electric light reminded her... Three years ago, the envious women in her village had spread a rumour about her shortly after the Survey Camp. They had gone around telling each other that the electric light burned all night long in the courtyard of Birju's mother. And, in that courtyard, you could hear the sound of an iron-soled boot as clearly as the hoof of an iron-shod horse... 'Burn! Burn! Burn with envy!' That's what she had said then. These very same women who had then burnt with envy at the sight of the silvery fibres drying in her courtyard, would turn into cinders now at the sight of the golden rice standing ready for harvest in her fields.

Champiya appeared, licking the date palm jaggery dripping from the earthenware pitcher. She yelped with pain as her irate mother slapped her. 'Why do you hit me? The shopkeeper took too long to serve me.'

'Was that the only shop in the entire village, or is it so special that you go there to get stuck? Speak up! I will kick you so hard that I will break your neck if I ever catch you singing "*And the flute plays no more...*" I know you go to learn these tricks and tunes from the "station girls"...'

Birju's mother was quiet for a minute as she tried to ascertain whether her voice had traveled till Jangi's hut.

Birju had forgotten past hurts. He had shaken the dust off his body and was now eyeing the jaggery dripping from the pot with greedy eyes. Had he too gone to the shop with his sister, he could also have had a lick of the jaggery. He had stayed back in the hope of getting a sweet potato, but his mother had smacked him several times instead!

'Ai Mai, give me a bit of the jaggery!' Birju whined as he spread out his palm. 'Please, mother, just a little bit!'

'Why just a little bit; I will go and dump the entire pot in the backyard and you can go and lick it all off the ground... I won't make any sweet roti now; you don't deserve it.' Birju's mother put the boiled sweet potatoes in front of Champiya, who was still crying, and said, 'Sit down and peel these, or else I will...'

Ten-year-old Champiya knew that her mother would scream and pull her hair at least twelve times while she sat and unpeeled the sweet potatoes, and abuse her over the smallest things. 'Why are you sitting with your legs stretched out, you shameless thing?' Champiya knows her mother's anger well enough.

Birju tried to please her by saying, 'Shall I also sit down and peel a few sweet potatoes?'

'No!' the mother spoke sternly. 'You will peel one and put away three in your tummy. Go and tell Sidhu's wife that she had borrowed my wok for an hour and has still not returned it. Go! Hurry!'

Poor, woebegone Birju looked at the sweet potatoes and jaggery longingly as he began to sidle out of the courtyard. Champiya peeped at her mother through her thatch of hair and quickly lobbed a sweet potato towards her brother... Birju caught it and ran!

'The Sun God has gone down. It is time to light the lamps and there is still no sign of the cart...'

Champiya piped up, 'No one from the Koyri[3] Tola gave their cart. Bappa wanted me to tell you to be ready... He was going to get a cart from Miyan Jaan of Maldahiya Toli.'

Birju's mother's face fell at these words. She felt a sudden jolt as though the stirrups had fallen off the horse. No one from the Koyri Tola was willing to give their cart. So now there was no hope of getting one! If there is no trace of cooperation from one's own village folk, how could one rely upon getting a cart from Miyaan Jaan of Maldahiya Toli? What was the point of getting ready? Why bother unpeeling the sweet potatoes? 'Put them away, Champiya! ... Do you think this man will take me to see the dance? That

[3] A sub-caste of cultivators, to which Birju's family belongs.

too on a bullock cart? I can dream on… of going to see the dance and that too on a bullock cart! By now all those who had gone on foot would be veterans of the dance!'

Birju returned with the upturned wok on his head. 'See, see… Look at my military hat. Nothing will happen to it even if you hit it ten times with a stick.'

Champiya sat quietly. She didn't utter a word; she didn't even smile. Birju understood: their mother was still angry.

Birju's mother grumbled as she shooed the billy goat out of the courtyard, 'You ogre, I am going to hand you over to the butcher tomorrow! You eat up everything in sight. Champiya, tie it up! And untie the bell from its neck… it drives me mad with its tinkling *tunur-tunur.* I don't like it one bit!'

The mention of the tinkling bell reminded Birju of the bullock carts that trundled past their house. 'The carts from the Babuan Tola went past just a minute ago. Did you hear their bells go *jhunur-jhunur…*'

'Don't talk so much,' cautioned Champiya as she untied the bell from the goat's neck.

'Champiya, pour water on the fire. Tell your father when he comes that he can go on his flying machine to see the dance. I am not crazy about any dance… And no one should wake me up! I have a headache.'

Birju whispered from the far end of the courtyard, 'Will there be flying machines too at the dance?'

Champiya, sitting on the mat with a patchwork quilt over her, gestured her brother to come and sit quietly beside her, or else he would get another whack from their mother.

Birju snuggled under the patchwork quilt beside his sister and sat with his chin on his raised knees. He has learnt to sit like this with his sister because it keeps him warm in the winter. He took his mouth close to Champiya's ear and said, 'Won't we go to see the dance? … There isn't a bird left in the entire village. Everyone has gone.'

Champiya didn't have an iota of hope left. The evening star was about to disappear and their father had still not returned with a cart. Their mother had been saying for the past month that she would make sweet roti on the day of the Balrampur dance—Champiya would wear a chintz sari and Birju would wear a pant, and they would ride on the bullock cart…

A tear drop quivered on Champiya's wet lashes.

Birju too felt close to tears. In his heart he vowed to offer one brinjal to the Djinn Baba who lived on the tamarind tree—the very first brinjal that ripened on the plant Birju had planted and watered with his own hands…. 'Djinn Baba, please send my father quickly with a cart!'

Birju's mother lay tossing and turning on her mat. 'Huh, never, never should one make plans for anything! God destroys all one's plans.' She wanted to ask God why she was being punished and where she had done wrong? She had never knowingly withheld any offering due to any god or goddess. All the offerings she had promised at the time of the Land Survey had been made… 'Oh my God! The sweets promised to Mahavirji were yet to be offered! Oh Mahavirji, forgive me! I shall offer twice the promised amount.'

Again and again, Jangi's daughter-in-law's words haunted Birju's mother… the taunt about the electric light jabbed her heart. But, after all, she consoled herself, won't the daughter and daughter-in-law of those who steal and pilfer be envious of her good fortune? Ever since Birju's father had been allotted five *bigha*s of land, it was as though the jealous village folk had got grit in their eyes! They looked at the jute in his fields and burned with envy. The crop looked like it had burst forth from the land; it was massed and heavy like the clouds in *Baisakh*. Can any harvest bear the brunt of so many envious eyes? This time only ten *mann* jute was weighed in at Rabbi Bhagat's weighing house, compared to the fifteen last year.

Why should there be any cause for resentment? Birju's father had tried his best to explain to everyone in the Kurmi Tola that as the time for the Survey was approaching, they ought to make the most of it if they didn't want to end up as petty labourers for the rest of their lives. 'Get smart, get tough and you can get a few *bigha* of land for yourselves too,' he had told them. And no one had had the courage to even cough in defiance of the Survey's Babu Sahab… And what of Birju's father? How much had he had to endure? How Zamindar Sahab had roared like a lion in a circus! His elder son had even come to their home and threatened to set it on fire. Finally, Babu Sahab had sent his younger son, who addressed Birju's mother as 'Aunty' and said, 'My father had bought this land in my name. My studies are funded by the crop that grows on this land…' He had gone on and on, saying several such things. That chit of a lad knew the art of sweet talking. After all, he was the son of a zamindar…

'Champiya, has Birju gone to sleep? Come here, Birju, come inside now. You, too, Champiya… Let that good man, your father, come… I will…'

Birju and Champiya went indoors.

'Snuff out the light… And don't answer when your father calls. Pull the screen down.'

'Good man! And what a good man he is! Just look at him… what would he have done if I hadn't nagged him into getting the land? He used to come home everyday, clutching his head and moaning that he didn't want the land, and that he was better off as a labourer. And how she used to tackle him in her clear-headed way! She would say, 'Fine, if you can't make up your mind and stick to your resolve, then what's the point? After all, don't they say that land and woman stay with the strong, or they go to those who are strong!'

Birju's father was quick to rouse to anger… And once he got angry, his anger only steadily got worse… Birju's mother bemoaned her fate at being stuck with such a good-for-nothing. Had he ever given her any happiness? She had spent her entire life working away like a pack mule… Had her husband bought her even a paisa's worth of *jalebi*?... He had taken the money from Rabbi Bhagat's weighing house and gone straight to the animal *haat;* he hadn't even let her catch a glimpse of the currency notes... He had gone and bought a pair of bullock. And from that very day, word had spread around the village like a wildfire—this year Birju's mother will go to see the dance on a bullock cart! ... He would take her to see the dance on someone else's cart, will he?

In the end, she got angry with herself. She was no better. May her tongue catch fire! God knew at which ill-omened hour she had expressed the desire to go to the dance on a bullock cart! And then, from the morning till the afternoon, she had mentioned the subject of going on the bullock cart no less than eighteen times! ... Now see the dance! And what a dance! ... Dreaming of soft shawls while cowering under tattered quilts! ... Tomorrow, when all the village women go to fetch water, that sharp-tongued daughter-in-law would come laughing, and go away laughing. Everyone was envious of Birju's mother. She had remained the same even after bearing two children. Her husband was under her control. She put coconut oil in her hair. She had her own land. Did anyone in this village own even an inch of land? Why wouldn't they envy her? She had three *bigha* of land planted with tender green paddy... if only it were to stay unharmed by their evil eyes.

The sound of bells worn by bullocks could be heard outside. The three of them inside the hut became instantly alert. They listened intently.

'It sounds like the bells of our bullocks, doesn't it, Champiya?'

Champiya and Birju answered in unison, 'Yes.'

'Quiet!' hissed Birju's mother. 'Can you hear the trundle of the cart?'

'Yes,' the two chorused again.

'Quiet! It isn't a cart. Make a hole in the screen and go take a quick look, Champi. Go quickly, run, but go softly.'

Champiya ran like a cat, soft-footed and soundlessly, to the screen. She peered through it and reported, 'Yes, mother, there is a cart too.'

Birju got up with a start. His mother pulled him down and patted him back to sleep, 'Hush, don't say a word!'

Champiya too snuggled in beside her mother.

The sound of a bullock cart being un-tethered could be heard outside. Birju's father scolded the pair of bullocks in a loud voice, 'Yes, yes, we have finally reached home. We were in such a hurry to get home, weren't we?'

Birju's mother was quick to cotton on. Surely he had smoked a pot full of *ganja* in the Maldahiya Toli. That accounts for the sharp ring in his voice!

'Champi-ya-aa!' he called out from outside. 'Give the bullocks their grass, Champiya.'

There was no answer from inside. Champiya's father stepped inside the courtyard and saw no light in the lamp, and no fire in the cooking area... What was going on? Eager to see the dance, had his wife set off on foot?

There was a rasping in Birju's throat and he did his best to suppress it, but once the coughing fit started, it lasted a full five minutes.

'Birju! Brijmohan, my son,' the father cooed. 'Has your mother gone to sleep in a fit of fury? ... People are still going to see the dance.'

Birju's mother wanted to make a crackling reply, 'I don't want to go; return the cart.'

'Champiya! Why aren't you getting up? Here, keep this posy of green rice stalks,' he said, putting the bunch of tender paddy on the thatch of their hut and calling out, 'Light the lamp.'

Birju's mother came out and said, 'What's the use of getting the cart past midnight? The dance must be coming to an end by now.'

In the flickering light of the oil lamp, she took one look at the tender green shoots of paddy and all the ill will in her heart melted away. The soft, vivid green seeped into her eyes and entered every pore of her body.

'The dance wouldn't even have started by now. Just a short while ago the Balrampur theatre company's cart had gone to fetch the big boss of the Mohanpur Hotel Bungalow. It is the last dance show this year... Stick the posy of rice stalks in the screen at our front door; it's from our field.'

Our field? Birju's mother asked, happiness lacing her voice, 'Has the paddy ripened?'

'No, but by the time *Agahan* begins—in the next ten days—the grain will turn red, and the ripened ears will begin to make the plants droop their heads... I was on my way to the Maldahiya Toli when I passed by my field and my eyes were glued to the sight. I tell you, my fingers were trembling when I was making this posy for you.'

Birju plucked a milky grain from the green stalk and put it in his mouth. His mother scolded him gently, 'What a greedy hog you are! As it is, our enemies are going to leave virtually nothing for us!'

'What happened? Why do you scold him?'

'Didn't you see? He ate the new rice without the *navvaan*[4].'

'They are exempted from all this... they are like little birds.'

'Make sure both don't put it in their mouth before the *navvaan.*'

But by then Champiya too had plucked two grains of rice from the green stalks and placed it between her teeth. 'Oh, Maiya! It is so sweet!'

'And it is so fragrant too, isn't it, Didiya!' Birju said as he put in more kernels in his mouth.

'Have you finished your cooking?' Birju's father asked with a smile.

'No,' Birju's mother answered in a tone laden with dignity. 'There was no knowing whether we were going or not... How could I cook under the circumstances?'

[4] Ceremony observed on first eating new rice or new grain fresh from the harvest.

'What an odd lot you are? Do you think someone who has bullocks won't get a cart on loan? After all, those who own the carts might need the bullocks one day. I will talk to the people from Koyri Tola some day and set them right... Come on now, get the food ready quickly!'

'Won't we get late?'

'Arre, you can make a basketful of roti in the blink of an eye; how long can it take you to make five rotis?'

Now a smile bloomed fully on Birju's mother's face. She looked from the corner of her eyes and saw Birju's father gazing adoringly at her. If Birju and Champiya had not been around, he would have laughingly declared his heartfelt intentions by now. Birju and Champiya looked at each other and their faces gleamed with happiness... Their mother was needlessly getting angry, wasn't she?

'Champi! Go and call out to Makhni Phua.'

'Ai Phua-a-a! Can you hear me, Phua-a-a-a? My mother is calling you.'

Phua made no answer, though her mumbling could be heard clearly, 'Yes, yes, why call out to Phua now? After all, she is the only one in the entire neighbourhood without a nose ring or a tether, isn't she?'

'Ari Phua,' Birju's mother laughed as she answered, 'Did you get offended by my words? Come and see my man with the bullock's nose ring and tether... He has brought the cart now that it is past midnight. Come Phua, come and help me make the sweet roti. I don't know how to make it.'

Phua came, coughing and clearing her throat. 'That is why I was asking you in the afternoon: "Won't you go to see the dance show?" Had you told me then, I would have lit my stove here and had a fire going long ago.'

Birju's mother showed Phua her cooking stove and said, 'We haven't stored any grain or rice in the house; there is only a billy goat and a few pots and pans. I will leave a good stock of tobacco to last you the night. Bring your *hukkah* and stay here, Phua.'

Phua didn't need anything else if she were promised a night's supply of tobacco. Why one night, she was ready to stay awake and keep watch for several nights. Phua felt the pouch of tobacco in the dark and tried to ascertain its size. Oh-ho… Birju's mother had given her a generous portion of tobacco. What a contrast from that grocer's wife! By God, that night she had gone off to the Gulab Bagh Mela giving her a pea-sized pinch of tobacco, as though it were a ball of opium, and told her it was a pouch full!

Birju's mother began to set the stove going. Champiya mashed the sweet potatoes while Birju wore the wok upside down on his head and showed off before his father, saying, 'Military hat! Nothing will happen to it even if you hit it ten times with a stick.'

Everyone burst out laughing. Birju's mother said gaily, 'There are a couple of plump sweet potatoes in the niche there. Give them to Birju, Champiya; the poor thing has been asking for them all evening…'

'Don't call him a poor thing; he is very clever,' now Champiya too began to chirrup gaily. 'You don't know why his mouth was moving under the patchwork quilt!'

'Hee-hee-hee.'

A voice spoke from between rows of half-broken milk teeth, 'The Black Martin has eaten five sweet potatoes. Haa-haa-haa!'

Everyone laughed uproariously again. To keep Phua in good humour, Birju's mother asked her, 'There is a pitcher of jaggery; shall I pour all of it, Phua?'

Pleased no end, Phua answered, 'The sweet potato is sweet too; why should you put so much jaggery?'

By now the two bullocks had eaten their fodder and drunk enough water, and were busy licking each other's body. Birju's mother got dressed. Champiya wore her chintz sari and Birju wore his pants, with a button missing and, therefore, tied up with a length of jute fibre.

Birju's mother stepped out of the courtyard and cocked her ears in the direction of the village, trying to catch any sound, 'Uh-huh, those who have to go on foot wouldn't have stayed so late.'

The full moon was nearly overhead. Birju's mother wore a real silver *maang tikka* for the first time ever… What has happened to Birju's father today? Why doesn't he yoke the bullocks to the cart? Why does he gaze at Birju's mother like that, as though the Queen of Hearts from the dance show is…

A quiver ran through Birju's mother's body as she got into the cart. She held the bamboo railing with one hand and called out, 'There is plenty of space in the cart; take your bullocks by the road on the right.'

As the bullocks began to run and the wheels began to squeak and then rumble loudly, Birju could contain his excitement no longer, 'Make it fly, Bappa, like a flying machine!'

The cart reached Jangi's backyard. Birju's mother told her husband, 'Find out if Jangi's daughter-in-law has left or not?'

The sound of someone crying inside Jangi's hut could be heard clearly the moment the cart came to a standstill. Birju's father asked, 'Arre Brother Jangi, what is all this crying and weeping?'

Jangi was warming himself beside a fire. He said, 'Don't ask. Rangi hasn't yet returned from Balrampur; how can his wife go without him? All the other women have gone by now.'

'Hey you, station girl! Why do you cry?' Birju's mother called out. 'Get dressed and come quickly! See, half the cart is empty! … You poor thing! Come! Come quickly!'

Sunri, Radhe's daughter, called out from the hut next door, 'Kaki, is there place in the cart? Can I come too?'

Larena Khwas lived on the other side of the bamboo grove. His wife too hadn't left yet. She came looking resplendent in her tin-plated ear rings and bangles.

'Come, come! All those who haven't gone yet can come along.'

Jangi's daughter-in-law, Larena's wife, Radhe's daughter—all three came near the bullock cart. One of the bullocks kicked its hind leg. Birju's father swore at the animal, 'You wretch! You will kick and make the girl lame, will you?'

Everyone laughed out loud. Birju's father looked at the two married women, their heads drooping under their veils. He was reminded of the drooping heads of paddy in his field.

Jangi's daughter-in-law had come from her parent's home barely three months ago. Her bright wedding sari still gave off the strong smell of mustard oil and vermillion. It reminded Birju's mother of the sari she had worn while leaving her parents' home. She opened a cloth bundle, produced three sweet rotis and said, 'Here, each one of you... eat one of these. Later, you can drink water from the government well at Simraha.'

The bullock cart emerged from the village and began to skirt the paddy fields at the outskirts. A moonlit night in the month of *Kartik*... The air was heavy with the scent of falling rice flowers. Somewhere, in the bamboo groves, a *dudhi*[5] vine was in full blossom. Jangi's daughter-in-law lit a *beedi* and passed it to Birju's mother. Birju's mother suddenly remembered: in the entire village it was only Champiya, Sunri, Larena's wife and Jangi's daughter-in-law, who knew how to sing the 'bioscope songs'... Nice!

The bullock track ran through the paddy fields. In every direction, there was a rustling—a bit like the rustling of a bridal sari... Moonlight was dappled across the *mang tikka* on Birju's mother's forehead.

'Sing us a song from the bioscope, Champiya! ... Why are you scared? In case you forget, you have your teacher sitting right there beside you!'

The two married women remained quiet but Champiya and Sunri cleared their throats.

[5] A kind of Asclepias, a plant with a milky juice.

Birju's father goaded the bullocks, 'Come on, brothers! Faster, faster! ... Sing, Champiya, or I will tell the bullocks to slow down!'

Jangi's daughter-in-law brought her veil-covered face close to Champiya's ear and whispered something, and Champiya slowly began to sing, '*The moon's light...*'

Birju's mother, sitting with Birju in her lap, wished she could join in too. She looked at Jangi's daughter-in-law; she too was humming softly. What a sweet girl she is! The bridal sari gave off a special sort of fragrance. And the girl was right about her, after all. Birju's mother is a queen; she is the Queen of Hearts. It isn't a bad thing to say about someone. After all, she truly is the Queen of Hearts.

Birju's mother tried to squint down at herself to see how she looked. She wore a red sari with a glittering border. On her forehead a moon-like *mang tikka* glimmered... Birju's mother harbours no other dreams in her heart now. She is feeling sleepy.

The Testimony

Ganpat was plucking piping hot potatoes from the pot of boiling rice and peeling them, when someone cleared his throat to signal his presence outside the door; in fact, it was not so much a signal as a warning. Ganpat called out: 'Who is there?'

'Who is inside? Is it you, Ganpatji?... Why is it dark in the office? Would you bring a lantern here, please?'

Ganpat was surprised. When did Comrade Balram return from Patna? The other comrades had still not returned from the rally; how and why had Balram come back?

Ganpat covered the boiled potatoes with a plate and came out with a lantern.

'Red Salute, comrade! How was the rally?'

Seeing Balram's long face, Ganpat's spirits plummeted. The solemn features did not bode well.

'Could you just open the office?'

Ganpat said to himself, 'Why "just"? I will open it "fully". How he frowns as he speaks... God knows what happens to these comrades after a single visit to Patna!'

He opened the door to the hut called 'the office'. The musty smell of stale air rushed out to greet them. The lantern's flame dipped a couple of times and began to tremble.

Balramji asked with a further tightening of his features, 'Does the lantern contain oil or water? Why don't you buy a chimney for it?'

Ganpat remembered his dinner of boiled rice. He couldn't stomach cold rice; it always gave him 'wind'. Lighting the small lamp in the kitchen he said, 'You ask of oil and chimney, comrade? Let me first have my meal, I will answer you later. If you want tea, I will put the pot to boil. There is some fire still left in the stove. And I have some tea leaves and even a Chinese lemon.'

Ganpat put a blackened aluminum pot on the stove and stoked the embers to life. Then he went back to peeling the potatoes. Mashed potatoes with hot rice... there is nothing more tempting than that for Ganpat in the whole world. Kusmi teases him sometimes by calling him 'rice-hungry man'. And Ganpat laughingly calls her 'husband-hungry woman'. He remembered how Balramji had cleared his throat to herald his presence outside the door. Had Kusmi been inside with him, Ganpat would have gone red in the face and made a feeble pretense of scolding poor, hapless Kusmi: 'If you don't feel like working, don't work here. You are as lazy as your good-for-nothing son.' And Kusmi would have laughed behind her veil and whispered...

As he mashed the potatoes, Ganpat recalled the headlines in the morning's newspaper: 'Our soldiers have beaten the enemy's tanks to a pulp...'

He added oil, chilly, onion and chopped coriander to the pulpy potatoes. As he spooned out the steaming rice on his gleaming brass *thali*, its fragrance seeped into every pore of his body. He remembered the first time he had experienced this palate-tickling aroma in 1930—at the volunteers' camp. Since then Ganpat had eaten at countless ashrams, camps, rallies, assemblies and jailhouse messes, but rice is not the same everywhere.

Ganpat ate his fill, washed his plate and cleaned the kitchen. In the morning Kusmi would re-plaster the crude stove with fresh clay. He called out to Kusmi's son, 'Shobhitlal! Take away the rice...'

Then Ganpat took out a cup from a wooden chest and made lemon tea for Balramji. With a pinch of roasted fennel clenched under one cheek, he entered the office with the teacup in one hand. Save for this after-dinner pinch of roasted fennel, Ganpat had no cravings. He neither smoked *beedi*s or cigarettes, nor chewed *paan* or tobacco.

Balramji's set features relaxed a little with the first sip of tea. Putting papers and documents into his leather folder, he asked, 'Why do you cook yourself? What does Shobhit's mother do?'

Ganpat knew how to read meaning in this obscure speech. He knew that he was actually being asked: 'Why are three rupees a month being given to Shobhit and a monthly salary of five rupees to his mother?'

Balramji fired his next salvo, 'Then? ... Have you collected any funds recently, or...'

Ganpat belched and said, 'As I was going to tell you, comrade...'

Balram stopped him mid-sentence and demanded, 'Why must you address me as comrade in every sentence?'

'What else do I call a comrade? In any case, what is new about it? Ever since I took the party's pledge in 1930, I have been calling everyone "comrade"...'

'That was then. No one says "comrade" anymore. No wonder people laugh when you speak.'

'What is there to laugh at?'

'All right, let's not argue. Who can win against you? So, what were you saying about the fund-raising?'

'What is there to say? The amount owing to the moneylender has shot up to 250 rupees in the past six months. The 50 rupees owing to the station *marwadi* since the last district rally have still not been paid. There was some hope of collecting funds after last year's crops, but then the famine struck. Who can ask for donations at such a time and who has money to give away? Since the new wheat is being planted this month, all the comrades have fled.'

Startled, Balram asked, 'Fled? Who has fled?'

Ganpat smiled and said, 'Fled not as in having gone fugitive; they are simply not here, that is all.'

Balram looked grave. He rose and said, 'You are right, Ganpatji. It seems as though everyone will flee.'

'What do you mean?'

'What good will it do you to understand what I mean? How can you comprehend this high-level, ideology-based struggle?'

Whatever else he might or might not understand, Ganpat well knew how to read a man's innermost thoughts. He smelt a whiff of something strange in Balramji's words... like the pungent smell of rancid oil in mashed potatoes.

High-level indeed! Illiterate Balram peppered his speech with many English words like capitalist, bourgeois, proletariat, clique, Gandhi-ite, peace, party literature and many more.

Balramji was not the only one among the 'new comrades' who thought Ganpat was worth no more than three cowries. Had Comrade Ziauddin or Shailendra or Gopalji been alive, would they have returned from a rally or meeting like Balram and others of his ilk—with a grim face and raised temper and loud words—to return to sleep beside their wives? Ever since the arrival of his wife, office secretary Balramji closes the office before sunset and hurries home.

*

For the past many years, Ganpat has been feeling something ominous darkening and settling down over everything. All around him, he sees people with no elation, no exultation in their hearts. Has the disease struck his party too? He will certainly raise the subject at the district meeting this year.

He knows that the moment he gets up to ask this question, the Johnny-come-lately comrades will start smiling and whispering among themselves and coughing their mock-coughs. Some might even call out, 'Comrade Ganpat, you must raise this question on the stage at the time of the cultural programme!'

'Hmm! On the stage, huh…'

Ganpat does not need to count on his fingers. He has done his calculations. Thirty-five years ago, he had stood on the stage of the Arya Samaj assembly, with a tambourine in one hand, to sing the song of the untouchables.

The memory of Parbatiya goes hand in hand with the memory of that assembly. Lovesick young Ganpat had kissed the mouth of a low-caste girl, though custom dictated that he ought not to even drink water touched by her hand. He had vowed that he would forsake everything for her sake. His family had joined hands with his entire community to torment him till, finally, he had turned to the minister of the Arya Samaj for help. But, by then, Parbatiya's father had left the village with his family—no one knew where.

After that Ganpat too left his home—never to return. He cut off all ties with his father, mother, brothers, sisters, the entire clan and village community, to devote himself to the country and its people. At every public gathering, Ganpat could be found, tambourine in hand, singing: '*O Hindus, think with your heart/ Think awhile/ Why this hatred for your brother…*'

In 1930 he had been jailed for singing this song. In the jail he had met Sarmaji and became a comrade under his influence. Sarmaji had chopped off his sacred lock of hair and refashioned his *janeo* to serve as a drawstring for his pajamas. He had said, 'You are Comrade Ganpat from now on. You don't need a tailpiece of Singh or any other appendage. You are a comrade; that is all.'

He remembered how his friends had mocked him. He, in turn, had riled them by asking the question Sarmaji had taught him: 'How will we get Self Rule through spinning the wheel and drinking goat's milk? Do explain.'

For many years after leaving the jail, Ganpat had been the only 'party comrade' in the entire district. He had lent his support to several branches of the Bihar-state peasant and labour unions. He had shouted slogans. He had picketed and fasted. He had played his tambourine and instead of the save-the-untouchable song of old, he had sung the new 'international song' Sarmaji had taught him: '*The sun is rising/ The red, red sun/ Wake, O peasant, wake/ Wake, O labouring brother, wake...*'

Child of Vaishnav parents, Ganpat had been a Vaishnav by birth, a slave of the womb. Yet he passed every test that Sarmaji had put him through. A vegetarian by birth, he had eaten an egg and even managed a *murgh mussallam* without a moment's hesitation or the slightest quiver of distaste. Sarmaji had praised him by saying, 'Well done, Ganpat. You are a revolutionary by birth...'

How can these school and college dropouts understand the meaning of comradeship? In his days there would be two pajamas, three half-pants and one *dhoti* between seven comrades. And they used to manage quite well among themselves. They would live on *sattu* for weeks. And now... now comrades are ready to launch a revolution at mealtimes during a rally. 'What is this? Special food for some and crumbs for the rest? This is an outrage! Down with injustice!'

If you ask a comrade to announce a rally without first providing a jeep or loudspeaker, you get the angry retort: 'Do you take me for a town-crier?' Comrades are ashamed of making announcements for their own causes. If they march with the party flag, they think it is a big comedown. Ganpat has lost count of the number of times he has beat a drum and announced: 'Brothers! Today, at four o'clock, come for removing poverty from the country, for destroying capitalists and putting the peasant and labourers in positions of power...'

And, if it hadn't been for Ganpat, would they have set up the 'Peasant Martyrs Ashram' in the village? No 'worker' of any party had ever dared to even cough in this area—such was the dread of its three tyrannical zamindars. After passing a resolution to launch the peasant's struggle for 800 acres of the land belonging to the three zamindars—brutes who could kill a man and make his corpse disappear without a trace—the party had sat silently for months. No brave comrade or revolutionary peasant ever dared step forward. It was Ganpat who took up the cudgels. For his pains, he was beaten up by the zamindars' men and left for dead. But he didn't die. From his hospital bed, he gave the rallying cry: 'Long live the peasants' movement! Long live the peasants of Bisanpur!' Had Ganpat not been wounded that day and rushed to hospital, the Peasants' Board would never have taken notice of the matter. Having won 800 acres of land for free, the peasants of Bisanpur, as a token of their appreciation, donated two acres to set up the Ashram—that too, after much pushing and prodding.

And now, come harvest time, comrades from all over the district, swarm to the Ashram, bags in hand, to claim their share of the harvest—some need it to marry off a sister, others to meet their household expenses. Ganpat has to do what he can for the sake of the party comrades' honour.

The lantern spluttered and died. Ganpat suddenly remembered a line from a *nirguna bhakti* poet: '*O fool, your life has passed in vain…*'

That night Ganpat dreamt that a thief was running away with the box from the party office. He tried calling out: 'Thief! Thief!'

The dream turned out to be true.

In the morning Comrade Chandrikaji arrived with the bad news: 'The party has been split in two!' The words struck him like bolts of lightning. Then he found that papers, documents, fund ledgers, receipt vouchers, stamps, everything had disappeared from the office. Ganpat said, 'Comrade Balram had come here last evening…'

He had not finished speaking when Comrade Chandrikaji's hand struck him across his face. Stung, he wanted to speak out in his defense when Comrade Chandrikaji started shouting, 'What on earth are you supposed to be doing here… collecting funds and filling your belly? Don't you know Comrade Balram is with the dissident members of the party? Huh?'

'I didn't know that,' Ganpat said briefly. 'I don't know who is a rebel and who is a supporter.'

'You are a traitor,' Chandrika pointed an accusing finger in his direction as though aiming a pistol at him. 'You have deceived the party. You are a cheat.'

Each insult, sharper and more penetrating than the other, pierced Ganpat like an arrow sinking deeper and deeper into his flesh. A crowd had collected... men, women and children from all over the village... Traitor! Deceiver! What damnation!

Comrade Chandrika delivered one last parting shot: 'I don't care what happens later; I am sacking you right now. Please leave.'

Comrade Balram arrived soon after. Ganpat could no longer control the tears that had been brimming in his eyes.

Balram said, 'Don't cry, Comrade Ganpat. We must face these dictators bravely. These children of the petit bourgeois had taken over the party as though it is their fiefdom.'

Ganpat spoke in a tremulous voice, 'Why did you do it, Comrade Balramji? If I had known you had come to take away office property, I would never have...'

Sudhir Mahto, the half-witted son of Akalo Mahto, spoke up, 'Ganpatji, you sink below the surface to drink water and you think no one can see you. The party office has not been made so that you can dally with widowed ladies.'

Ganpat was devastated. He had been ridiculed in front of the entire village by Sudhir Mahto. Not only had he been branded a cheat and a traitor, he was also declared a depraved man. What was left now to hear?

Balram thrust a bundle of red leaflets in his hand before leaving. 'These should be distributed at the *haat*, station, everywhere. Understood?'

Ganpat entered his hut and sprawled across his bed like a fallen tree. He could feel the abuses piercing his body. He reached out for one of the red leaflets and tried to read it. Several of the party bigwigs were warning the masses: 'Beware of the traitors who have tied the party to the purse-strings of the capitalists, in the name of peasants and workers...'

Ganpat could read no further. Mutual abuse, mud slinging... everything had gone awry. Ganpat could feel the bile rising in his stomach. Soon, gas would form. He could already feel the nausea.

Who is right, who is wrong? Comrade Chorghade or Comrade Jadav? Last year Chorghadeji had come to chair the district peasants' union. In the welcome address, Jadavji had praised him to the skies... All lies. Chorghadeji has called the Bihar party a flock of traitors in this leaflet.

Ganpat decided he would go to Patna, even Delhi if need be. He would meet big and small party members. He would cry, plead, talk of the plight of the common man. He would play his tambourine and sing: '*Don't go to the court with your quarrels...*'

Jadavji and Chorghadeji are fighting in front of the party office. Sword in hand, they attack each other. Ganpat comes forward and stands between them, saying, 'Peace! Please!' when both swords fall on his neck.

A scene from a play seen some fifteen years ago unfurls before his eyes and disappears abruptly. Shivers rack his body. He has malaria. He vomits, puts a pinch of roasted fennel in his mouth and lies down on his bed covered with a blanket. The shivering stops as the fever begins to rise. He becomes delirious. He has fallen ill for the first time in forty years, he who had not known even a headache in all these years. A feeble cry escapes his lips, 'Mother! Parbati...!'

He sees Sarmaji standing in front of him holding bright red apples and oranges. He takes out their juice and turns to Ganpat, 'Drink this, comrade. It will do you good.' Ganpat drinks and as the first sip slides down, he feels as though his throat is on fire. It is bitter poison.

Parbatiya comes. She sits at the foot of his bed and starts pressing his feet. Ganpat's parents appear, clicking their beads and glaring at Parbatiya.

Silkworkers' union. Strike at Bhagalpur. Tambourine in hand, Ganpat is leading the rally, shouting, 'Workers of the world, unite…'

The police burst tear gas shells. Soldiers on horseback jostle the crowd, thrashing them with their crops, trampling them underfoot and finally riding away in a cloud of dust.

Ganpat is lying in a filthy jail cell. A bandage is tied around his head. Parbatiya – Parbatiya – Parbatiya – Paro-o-o…!

*

The fever broke after seven days. Kusumi said, 'Doctor Babu took great care of you. He used to give you two injections every day.' And it was against this very doctor that Ganpat had distributed pamphlets, at Balram's insistence, announcing: 'The cruel doctor at Bishnupur hospital should be immediately sacked!'

Ganpat felt as though the fever had lasted not seven days but had had him in its grip for the past thirty-five years. He had been traveling in a blind tunnel all along, without meaning, purpose or destination.

Kusmi brought him a glass of puffed rice soaked in hot milk. 'Doctor Sahib has said you should eat *mangur* fish. I have sent Shobhit. I am sure he will be able to catch a *ser* or two by the evening.'

After a while, she continued, 'Every single person from the village has come in the past seven days to ask after you. But not one of your so-called comrades has so much as peeped in. Balram Babu informed me yesterday that I should take you home with me. The party office has to be vacated. You have been sacked.'

Rebel Ganpat, who had fought against his family, his caste, his religion, his community, against injustice and cruelty, now lay like a defeated wrestler in the ring. Everyone had kicked him in the butt, showered him with abuses and gone their way. For thirty-five years he had lived like an ascetic, put a lock on his tongue and mouth and heart, and devoted himself to the public cause. He had never touched a twig belonging to another, nor pocketed a paisa belonging to the party. He had loved the party and the party's flag more than his father and mother, brother and sister, village and community, even Parbatiya. All gone to waste…

Ganpat felt as though the sun and moon too had developed cracks. The entire world had been split into two. Every man had two halves, two faces and a cracked heart. All those things that he had always dismissed as the claptrap of capitalists, imperialists and war-mongers, rose to haunt him.

'Your leaders, Ganpat, and your party call religion the opium of the masses. But why don't your leaders ever marry their sons and daughters into other communities? Comrade Ramlagan Sarma took Rs 25,000 as dowry at the time of his son's wedding. Your leaders' children study in fancy schools in Darjeeling and Dehradun. The party secretary's wife indulges in factional politics to get a ministerial berth within the Congress party. And your Toofanji—he joined hands with the mill owners to exploit the poor workers…'

The portraits of all the great comrades rise before his eyes: Chorghadeji, Jadavji, Gopalji, Sinha Sahab, Thakurji, Toofanji. There is only one sentence on everyone's lips: 'We were on the wrong path.'

Ganpat has emerged from a blind tunnel and is lying lifeless. His graying moustaches droop on his ashen face. He has been traveling on the wrong road, in the wrong direction, for thirty-five years. Who knows how many mistakes he has made! God knows how many people he has misguided!

Had the seed in Parbatiya's womb not been aborted, the child would have been thirty-five years old now. Had it been a son, he would have been as old as Balram.

He had betrayed Parbatiya. His first mistake… for which he was paying till this day.

Kusmi has been showing every sign of being in love with Ganpat for the past five years. Ganpat understands, but pretends not to. Poor, widowed Kusmi can do little more than gaze at him with love in her eyes. And yet, Akalu Mahto's drunkard son had smirked and said, 'Dallying with widowed ladies!'

Kusmi fetched Bhartha, the barber. As he began to shave Ganpat, she said: 'Trim the moustache too; he has to slurp his milk and barley through it.'

Ganpat ate some rice with mashed potatoes and felt better. The rancid taste in his mouth lessened somewhat. He put a pinch of fennel in his mouth and looked at himself in the mirror… How strange! He looked exactly like an old horse whose forelegs had been shackled (thirty-five years ago!) by his heartless owner and who had been left to die on the streets. Now he lay on the ground, drawing his last breaths, moving his legs with the little energy he had left. Crows had pecked innumerable holes in his body. Parbatiya came running, with a sickle in one hand, and cut the ropes that bound his forelegs. Once the ropes were cut, the half-dead horse rose to his feet, bent his head and started sniffing the ground.

Ganpat stretched his legs slowly, gingerly.

Comrade Chandrika's voice could be heard outside. A policeman in a red turban peered inside Ganpat's hut and said, 'The peon can be seen lying on a mat on the floor.'

At the sight of the Darogha from the police post and his assistant, something began to seep into Ganpat's hollow empty frame. His nerves began to tingle. He looked towards Comrade Chandrika once. Darogha Sahab said, 'Look here, Ganpat, are you the Ashram's peon, or not?'

'Don't use that tone with me; I am no one's peon.'

The Darogha looked at Chandrika.

Chandrikaji spoke up, "Look, Ganpat, Darogha Sahab has come to clamp Section 144 on the Ashram. You…'

Ganpat was by now fully in control of himself. He spoke in a clear, unafraid voice, 'But where is the Ashram here? This is my home. Built on my land. This is not public property, nor is it a wrestler's pit for feuding political parties.'

The Darogha's assistant was trying to peer inside the hut. Ganpat spoke in a crackling tone, 'You, there! Why are you snooping in the women's quarter? Do you want to lose your job?'

Darogha Sahab asked in a milder voice, 'You, you... Do you have any proof of ownership?'

'Proof! What sort of proof? Written or oral? Witnesses? ... Shobhit's mother! Bring my bag here.'

Shobhit's mother, Kusmi, came out, her face heavily veiled, carrying the bag. Ganpat began to pluck his books and papers from the bag: 'The Essentials of Marxism', 'Songs of Workers and Peasants', 'The Song of the Cruel Zamindar', the famous proposal of Baijwada, 'The Red Goddess of Telangana', songs from the famous film 'Shaheed', 'Enemies of the Country', 'Democracy'... Here, here is your written proof. And now you want oral proof? You want verbal testimony? Go and ask any child from this village.'

Darogha Sahab straightened the scattered pages, smoothed them out and began to read them from beginning to end. Then he smiled and turned towards Chandrikaji and said, 'He is right... The property is registered in his name.'

Chandrikaji began to shout angrily, 'You cheat! You want to usurp public property? I shall see how you...'

Ganpat stood up. 'Don't take the public's name, Chandrika; the public is not blind, it sees everything, it understands everything. You, who have splintered the party for your own selfish interests...'

Kusmi's voice interrupted him from inside the hut, 'What's the point of bandying words with such people? The Doctor Sahab has said, hasn't he, you mustn't tire yourself. It's a case of "The bull gets himself killed in fights, while the horse sits around getting fat."'

Ganpat raised his voice, 'Long live the Revolution! Down with the Dissenters! Enemies of the party White-Collars!

A quiver of excitement rippled through the crowd that had gathered in front of Ganpat's hut. When people started shouting slogans along with Ganpat, Darogha Sahab made a quick exit. He said something to Chandrika in English as he was leaving.

The Darogha's assistant also added his bit, 'Sir, this looks like an internal matter of the party-*wallah*s. It won't be wise for us to linger; our presence will only make things worse.'

The crowd raised a jubilant cry after Chandrika and the Darogha had left. 'Say it with me once... Long live Ganpatji! Who is the leader of the peasants?... Ganpatji! Who is the leader of the workers?... Ganpatji! Victory to Ganpatji! He who clashes with us... will be smashed to smithereens!'

Ganpat was overwhelmed. For the first time in thirty-five years he had heard the rallying cry go up in his name. For the first time he had heard such jubilation—all directed towards him!

In the midst of all the excitement and chaos, someone launched into a speech: 'Brothers! This time, in the coming elections for the Gram Panchayat and the village headman's post, let us unite to defeat these no-good long kurta and pajama-clad jokers! ... Tonight, we shall have a grand feast for the peasants right here, on this very spot!'

When the crowd had dispersed and everyone had gone home, Ganpat called out, 'Shobhit's mother!... Come out for a minute.'

Kusmi came. She saw Ganpat's face and grew alarmed; had the fever returned? She touched his forehead. Ganpat held her wrist. His lips moved a little as he drew Kusmi's face close to his. Then he spoke in a trembling voice, 'Kusum... but this is a sin, an injustice, that too on public property, on the party's land, inside the Ashram... no, no, this is a sin, a wickedness...'

Kusmi liked the scent of fennel that wafted from Ganpat's mouth. She spoke in a voice laced with pride, 'Why is it a sin? Chandrika Babu got a *pucca* house built with the party's fund. Ramlagan Babu took bribes from the zamindars to screw up the litigation of the poor landless labourers. And...'

'Let others do as they will, Kusmi, but I cannot do this. If you want me to live, take me to your hut.'

Kusmi looked at Ganpat's brimming eyes and flushed face for a few seconds, then asked, 'And what of the Ashram?'

'I will return the land to the people. If ten people get together and give something, it is regarded as a deed gift. It can never bring happiness to the man who wants to enjoy it all by himself... And I can no longer work for the party, now that the party itself has broken up into parts...'

And he began to cry like a baby. Kusmi kept wiping his tears with the end of her grubby sari, murmuring, 'Don't cry, please don't cry...'

Ganpat crushed Kusmi against his chest. Aaah... the heat of a woman's breast rushed through his body like a tornado. He bent to touch Kusmi's dark lips with his own, then stopped.

'No, Kusmi, not here... let's go home. I don't have the right to stay here a minute longer.'

Kusmi got up. She took Ganpat's hand to help him up and said, 'Come.'

'Mother! Mother! Look... I have caught so much fish!'

Shobhit placed a cane basket in front of them. Several black *mangur* fish glimmered from the basket.

Kusmi said, 'Fish are good omen.'

Ganpat laughed.

Kusmi said to her nearly grown-up only son, 'Babua, help Kaka to his feet. You go ahead; I will bring the bedding and follow.'

Shobhit looked askance at his mother and asked, 'Where?'

Ganpat answered, 'Wherever you want, son.'

Ganpat turned to look back once. The faded and frazzled party flag fluttered in the wind. He felt he had become like the party flag, and was now being carried away by Shobhit on his young shoulders.

The Party's Ghost

> I am scared to face my friends, because, you see,
> What if they ask: which party do you belong to?

I have become thin as a rake. My eyes have sunk into deep pits. My hair is overgrown. My pajamas are torn. My slippers are broken. I look like a lovelorn Romeo. I find neither peace during the day, nor sleep at night. Perchance if I do sleep, I am woken up by nightmares. No, I don't suffer from the disease you probably have in mind. If I did suffer from that particular malady, I would at least have enjoyed the state of idleness and waiting that comes with it. My disease is the sort that is guaranteed to get me a ticket straight for Ranchi[1]. And as that day is not far, I consider it my duty to publish an account of my illness. Once that state of oblivion dawns, I shall not be able to give a coherent account. The fact of the matter is that I am haunted by the party's ghost. It has had me in its thrall from a very young age. Now it has left me a good for nothing.

Let me begin my story from my school days.

One day, I was sitting beside my father and reading a book. The teacher from the village school arrived. For a long time, he spoke

[1] A town in erstwhile Bihar, and now the capital of Jharkhand, Ranchi was once famous for its mental asylum.

of this and that, and then, baring his teeth in a huge ingratiating smile, he said, 'Whatever quarrels you might have, are amongst you people; I have nothing to do with your fights. All of you are important, respectable people. Just as there can only be one lion king in the jungle, in the village there cannot be two... *he-he-he*... it is the law of nature. But the school, however, isn't theirs (meaning, the opposite party's). I am there at the school; I make no difference between your children and theirs...'

'You don't understand, Panditji,' my father cut him short. 'The school is run by their party. Forget about my son, there are other boys in the village... If I am not able to send the other boys to school, it will bring shame to my party...'

The teacher once again bared his teeth in a smile and said, 'That is true... yes, it is... Believe me, I only want to serve you,' he coughed forcefully, looked around and began to speak more ingratiatingly than ever. As a result, the other boys from my village and I were granted permission to attend school.

The very next day I went to school with my friends. The news spread like lightning—across the neighborhood, in the entire village, among our extended clan, even in the Bar Library of the District Court. People began to ask all sorts of questions.

'Does this mean that the village will now be united?' the professional witness asked in a woebegone manner.

'Now they will start marrying among themselves; next, there shall be feasts and marriages,' the pillars of the community said with hungry anticipation.

'But what about the litigation that is underway? Will all these cases be withdrawn?' the lawyers asked worriedly.

But nothing happened. The party lines remained intact. In fact, the parties were formed in the school too. Petty fights, incidents of stone pelting and gang warfare would routinely break out after school. The teacher's cane tried to keep the peace as best as it could. I never took an active part in these fights and never got a taste of the cane, but I did pray for my party's victory. And I would give sage counsel. I was, therefore, regarded as a hero by 'my' boys.

As these quarrels continued unabated, a girl called Chandu came to our school. She was the only girl from the opposite party. That day I told my boys that there was nothing to be gained from this needless fighting. And all quarrels stopped thenceforth. The opposite camp made an occasional attempt to initiate a fight, but in the face of our disinterest they too gave up eventually.

Now that I have read a couple of books on the reproductive system, I can fully appreciate why I was so attracted towards Chandu. We didn't read about Laila and Majnu in our books, but I had read about the love story of Sanyukta and Prithviraj[2] in our history textbook. I wanted to win Chandu, like Prithviraj had won his Sanyukta. One day, when I found a moment alone with Chandu, I said, 'Chandu, in the story about Prithviraj and Sanyukta…'

'Don't talk to me! You belong to the other party. Go away!' she scolded.

'No, no, I don't belong to that party!' I whined.

'What?' she stopped and turned back.

'I belong to your party,' I said.

'Really?' she said as she stepped closer.

I grabbed her hand and said, 'Yes, really.'

[2] Prithviraj Chauhan, the warrior chieftain of Delhi, won the hand of Princess Sanyukta, daughter of King Jaichand of Kannauj, in a *swayamvar* to which he had not been invited, and this enraged her father. This led to a rift between the kingdoms of Delhi and Kannauj, and Sultan Muhammad Ghori of Afghanistan took advantage of this to defeat Prithivraj Chauhan in the second battle of Tarain in 1192. A dashing, romantic figure according to popular legend, Prithviraj was defeated by the Afghan invader due to the treachery of his own father-in-law, Jaichand. In popular perception, Jaichand is seen as a traitor who brought about the downfall of his own people.

Well-built Rajna, also the most quarrelsome boy in the school, had been hiding among some flower bushes. He came out, looked at me and hissed through clenched teeth, 'Traitor!'

My tale of Sanyukta and Prithviraj remained incomplete. Chandu pulled her hand out of mine and walked away. Even those who had read only the story of Shri Ram in their history books, began to call me Jaichand, and not Prithviraj.

I finished my studies in the village school and came to the city to enroll in a high school. Call it good fortune or bad luck, but my father's lawyer was a Bengali gentleman. He gladly accepted me into his family. As a result, not only did I make many good friends among Bengalis, I also began to take an active interest in Bengali literature and music. Within two or three years I began to wonder if I was a non-Bengali. A short while later, the battle between Bengalis and non-Bengalis erupted. Both sides were generous with abuses.

The non-Bengalis would say, 'The Bengalis are lowly cowards!'

The Bengali response would be, 'Turncoats and cheats!'

Angry non-Bengalis would then cross all limits. I would listen to the stream of abuses and shrivel up. *Chhee*! Such language! After all, Rabindranath, Jagdish, Sharat Chandra and Subhash too are Bengalis!

Well, the Bengalis were never slack in hitting back. The non-Bengali inside me would then reprimand the Bengali in me.

My Bengali friends had the following opinion of me: 'No matter what, he is an Indian and will remain an Indian.'

My non-Bengali friends twisted the knife in by saying, 'Have you now seen their friendship for yourself? Who is wicked, tell us…'

'Shut up!' I would say in exasperation.

'All right then,' the non-Bengalis passed a unanimous decision, 'We don't care for the abuses heaped upon us by the Bengalis because whatever they say or do is for the sake of regionalism. But a non-Bengali taking the side of Bengalis is a traitor, a turncoat, a Mir Jafar[3]. We wish to have nothing to do with such people.'

❦

The story of my college days is somewhat longer but certainly far more interesting.

Crowned by these epithets, I left school and entered college. I had already sworn not to get entangled in the web of regionalism.

The first year passed without mishap; I heard and saw everything, but took no active role in anything. In the second year, I decided to change my garb. I hadn't planned anything spectacular; I only forsook the dhoti for pajamas and got long kurtas stitched for myself, which had stiff inch-and-a-half collars. As a special treat, I decided to visit a cinema hall wearing my new clothes. On the tonga, when the man seated beside me asked my name, year, subjects, hostel, room number and then, 'So, which party do you belong to?', I panicked.

'Communist Party?' he smiled and asked.

'Yes,' I said, thinking it would all be over in the next five minutes.

'I see,' and he thumped me vigorously on my back. I nearly jumped with surprise.

'We are comrades. Don't be scared,' he put his hand over my shoulder and spoke lovingly.

[3] Mir Jafar had promised support to Siraj-ud-Daulah in the 1757 Battle of Plassey, but eventually stood by and watched the British rout the Nawab's forces. He succeeded Siraj-ud-Daulah as the eighth Nawab of Bengal, leading to the eventual British domination of the country. His name, therefore, became a byword for treachery and deceit. The word *mirjafar* in Bengali and the phrase '*meer jafar*' in Urdu are now synonymous with traitor, used much like *quisling* is used in English.

That day, not only did he settle the bill at the 'Kashmir Cabin', he also paid for the first class film ticket.

The next day my best friend Vinod came up to me as soon as I entered the class, and said with a huge grin, 'Wow! You look like a true Socialist!'

I said, 'You can say whatever you want.'

Vinod answered, 'No, you can't just say that; you must become one.'

'Become what?' I asked in surprise.

'A member! What else? I used to think you had no interest in party politics. But I can see you are no ignoramus.' And he began to smile again.

Till this day I cannot figure out why or how Vinod decided that I was sufficiently well grounded in party politics. Be that as it may, on the very day that my name was entered in the register of the Students Federation (Communist Group), I was informed that I had also been included in the Working Committee of the Students Federation (Socialist Group).

Had it been a matter of belonging to just two parties, it would not have been too worrying; but I soon got entangled with a third party.

One day, I was sitting and drinking tea in the 'Kyalkata Kafe' (as proclaimed by its signboard). In my hand I held a monthly Bengali journal. A young man, roughly the same age as me, sat beside me drinking tea. He looked closely at me and at the journal in my hands a number of times, and then asked, 'Are you a Bengali?' To escape being awarded the epithet of 'fraud', I quickly said, 'Yes'.

'Oh! You have come here to study? What are you studying?'

'Second Year Arts.'

'Good,' he said and called out to a group of young men sitting in a corner of the café arguing amongst themselves. 'Hey! Habu! Bhola! Kalu! Nilu! Phela! You haven't found anyone from Second Year Arts to join up as a member. Here, here's one…'

The others abandoned their arguments and came running to sit around me. They ordered tea and began an animated conversation.

They spoke of meeting regularly and stressed the importance of getting 'organised'. The funny thing was that I kept agreeing with everything they said, even though I didn't even know the name of their party. A youth stepped forward to have a word with the manager. He then came to me and spoke in a hushed tone, 'Concession from today! Do you get it? It's the party's cafe, after all. He didn't know that you belong to the Bloc.'

And from that day onwards, I began to get tea and cutlets at the 'Kyalkata Kafe' at a special rate debited to the Forward Bloc's account.

One Sunday I was lying in bed reading *Godan*[4] when Vinod came in a terrible rush and said excitedly, 'Hey, you member of the Working Committee! Do you know what's going on? Comrade Ram Pratap is coming at 4 pm! And there will be a rally in the park tomorrow... What are you reading? *Godan*? How silly!'

'Why is it silly?' I asked dumbfounded.

'It is a reactionary book!...Are you coming at four?' he said, and left in as much of a rush as he had come in. And I got to my feet and began to look up 'reactionary' in the dictionary.

I dressed with care in my new clothes and left at 3.30 pm. At the gate, a modern young lady was making enquiries from the gardener. I took stock of my appearance—from the tip of my *chappals* to my pajamas. The gardener took one look at me and exclaimed, 'That's

[4] Premchand's novel *Godan*. While Premchand inaugurated the First Progressive Writers' Seminar in Lucknow in 1925, and was well-regarded by the majority of the progressive writers for his socially engaged writing, to the Socialists his brand of literature was still mostly woolly claptrap. The only literature worth reading for them was the *Manifesto* and the texts and brochures produced by the party itself. Here, Vinod condemns *Godan* as being 'reactionary' because, by the 1950s, a certain section of the progressive intelligentsia had begun to berate Premchand for romanticising poverty and eulogising the rural hinterland and some of its traditions that, they felt, were dragging the nation backwards.

him!' The young lady came towards me with a smile, greeted me with a comrade-like salute, handed me a letter and said, 'Here's an urgent letter for you.' I opened the letter and read:

> The Socialist leader Ram Pratap is arriving. Our party has decided to greet him at the station at 4 pm with black flags. Please come immediately with Miss Rossa. Be ready at the platform with all your members. The moment the Punjab Mail arrives, you start shouting 'Down with Ram Pratap!' and wave your black flags.
>
> — The Secretary

As I finished reading the letter and raised my eyes to look at the messenger, a wave of pleasure coursed through my body like electricity. Never in my wildest dreams had I imagined that a beauty like Miss Rossa would gaze upon me so fondly! I blinked and looked again. Still smiling, she asked me in a tone as sweet as sugar, 'You are coming, aren't you?'

'Let's go,' I said, swaying like a drunk.

We got into a tonga and set off for the station. For a minute I recovered my senses enough to ask myself, 'What am I doing? Am I about to insult someone for whom I have immense respect? And that too, for no particular reason? No, no, I cannot do that.'

'You don't smoke?'

'Uh?'

'You don't smoke?'

'Uh... no, no I don't,' I came out of my reverie.

'What were you thinking of, comrade?' She asked, looking directly into my eyes.

'I was thinking... well, actually, I wasn't thinking of anything at all,' I muttered and immediately lowered my gaze.

'Go on, I don't believe you! Surely you were thinking of something. Why do you hide what is in your heart? Anyhow, it doesn't matter what you were thinking... tell me, you really don't smoke at all, do you?'

'At all, meaning, I do smoke occasionally... it is just that I am not habituated to it.'

'Well, then go ahead... smoke... please do,' she spoke almost beseechingly.

The tonga driver got off and got me a tin of cigarettes. She cut open the tin, pulled out a cigarette and lit a match with a flourish. I took a drag and asked, 'What about you?'

'I don't smoke,' she tilted her head back, striking a pose like a film star. I gaped.

'I can quite understand your surprise. The thing is, you see, I have very clear views on certain issues,' she said, with an ask-and-I-shall-tell look.

'Such as?' I asked, blowing smoke away from her.

'Why are you blowing the smoke in that direction?' she complained.

'Where should I blow it, then?'

'Blow it in my direction,' she said like an insistent child.

'Your direction?'

'Yes. I said just now that I have very clear views on certain issues, didn't I? Take cigarettes, for example. I can't imagine being in the company of a man who does not smell of cigarettes. Cigarettes are meant to be smoked by men, and the scent of its smoke is meant to be inhaled by women,' she pronounced her first opinion with the utmost gravitas. I began to drown in the philosophy of cigarettes. I forgot all about the world. She spoke again, 'I shall not tell you my second opinion.' And she immediately struck the I-am-angry-and-shall-stay-angry-till-you-placate-me pose.

'Please tell me,' I spoke with feeling.

'No, first you tell me what you were thinking of earlier.'

'I was thinking...'

'Yes, tell me...'

'What shall I say,' I looked at her and smiled.

'You are a real so-and-so! You are acting as though you are a fresh new recruit.'

'I was thinking that... I... you...'

'All right, that's enough. I have understood,' she said and burst into laughter. Suddenly, I was reminded of the world, the road, the pedestrians, the shops, the tonga driver. I looked around myself with new eyes.

'Why are you pretending to look around? You really know how to fool a person! You are trying to test me, aren't you? Listen, I will tell you my second opinion; it concerns beards. I don't believe men should shave everyday. The second-day stubble…'

I found this stubble philosophy a bit shallow after the cigarette-smoke philosophy. I hit the ground with a thud. 'My God!' unwittingly the words escaped me, but equally suddenly I remembered that we are Communists, and such is God's grace that I completed my sentence almost without a pause by saying, '…rej.'

'My Godrej? What does that mean?' she asked.

'Godrej? Godrej Number One… Key Trademark… Fully-Homegrown… Godrej Shaving Stick,' I said, thanking God for my presence of mind.

'Oh! You were reminded of the shaving stick when I spoke of shaving, were you? Do you use Godrej products?"

'Yes.' Exhausted by my quick thinking, I answered briefly.

'But…'

The tonga had reached the station by now. The tonga driver said, '*Huzoor*, the train has reached the platform.'

We found our seats. She handed me the tin of cigarettes before paying off the porter. I blew smoke out of the window as the train blew its whistle. I was immediately reminded of my mistake; apologising wordlessly, I contritely blew three or four puffs of smoke towards her face. Her eyes hid beneath the cloud of that sweetly cruel smoke, but her sharply pointed nose twitched with pleasure, sniffing the scent of tobacco.

The next day the train came to a halt at the platform early in the morning. And I, along with two dozen members of my party—mostly young men and women—raised the slogan, 'Down with Ram Pratap!' Fluttering black flags filled the platform.

'Ram Pratap is a toady of the Congress!' shouted Miss Rossa.

'Ram Pratap is a Congress poodle,' I added my bit.

Forget about shouting slogans and raising black flags, at Miss Rossa's bidding I would willingly have wrung someone's neck. The sloganeering was rising in pitch when, suddenly, the door of the train compartment opened. A man with a majestic countenance and a highly impressive personality stood in the doorway with a smile playing on his lips. You can say he had an innocent, almost pure smile.

'It is him, it is him,' Rossa said.

'Huh...'

'Down with Ram Pratap,' Rossa shouted.

The train moved. The man kept standing at the door, smiling.

'But there isn't the smallest strain on his face...' I began to say when Rossa cut me short, 'He's Gandhi's acolyte. These fellows have learnt all their tricks from Gandhi. They keep smiling even when they are being beaten with shoes. Shame on them! They are nothing but dyed-in-the-wool cynics and opportunists. Pretending to be socialists... Setting out to usher in revolutions... Huh! They are a bunch of frauds!'

By the time I reached the hostel, I was fearful of two things: one, that my friendship with Vinod would come to an end; and second, that his party would shower me with certain expected, time-honoured, long-memorised abuses. In a way, I would have been happy; I would have been rid of the lot. But nothing happened. Vinod came to me and merely upbraided me for not being there; then he went on to tell me how successful the rally had been.

Things continued like this for the next few months. Sometimes, I wanted to leave my studies midway and run away. After all, how could one continue to be a member of three parties and expect to keep one's honour intact!

If I considered sacrificing all other parties in favour of the credit offered at the 'Kyalkata Kafe', Miss Rossa's intoxicating eyes would come and stand in my way. One day, a member of the

Forward Bloc took me aside, handed me a handbill written in Bangla and entrusted me with the task of translating it in Hindi. I duly translated it. The same night, it was typed and printed. The next morning, I was on my way back from the *chowk* when I was accosted midway and two bundles of the handbill were wordlessly given to me. I would now have to get them distributed. And if I couldn't find volunteers, I would have to distribute them myself. It was the party's diktat. There was a time when one used to blindly obey one's parents; one had to jump to do their bidding. But in this scientific age, the party's orders take precedence over all else. In any case, it is the duty of all revolutionaries to break the rules laid down by their parents. So, regardless of whether these handbills contained the latest gossip or news about the atom bomb, I had to either get them distributed or do so myself.

The tonga had barely reached the third crossing, when a sweet voice reached my ears, 'Comrade!'

It was Miss Rossa! She got down from her tonga and got into mine, as though she had been looking for me and traveling in vain across hill and dale. We were both striking the right pose and getting set to start a serious conversation when, barely ten steps away, the tonga was stopped yet again. This was to be the last time the tonga would be stopped today. We were face-to-face with an inspector from the CID. He expressed great pleasure at seeing the two of us together and spoke with far more gentleness than the occasion warranted, 'Forgive me, but I must search both of you.'

There was a small police post nearby. We were both taken there. A thorough search was conducted. Several letters, written on scented paper, were recovered from Miss Rossa's handbag along with their envelopes. I stole a glance at one of the letters from the corner of my eye. It began: 'My Queen!' My heart had already been thudding; now the light began to fade from my eyes.

When the policemen turned towards the bundles, I sat down on a broken chair with a thud. The bundles were opened. The policemen grinned with delight, 'Here you are!'

'So, tell us, sir, these bundles were supposed to contain cosmetics and saris; where did these papers come from?' the inspector took a dig at us and smiled.

I stayed quiet. Miss Rossa had turned quite pale by now. A small shriek escaped her lips.

We were taken to the local jail. That Icon of Liberty and Revolution, Miss Rossa, began to blubber like a baby as she was led away to the Ladies' Wing. I reached my cell and drew a deep breath of relief.

The next day, a newspaper carried the following headline: 'Members of the Students' Federation (Communist Group), Comrades P Rai and Miss Rossa, were arrested carrying objectionable papers!'

Another newspaper carried this report: 'Comrade Prafull, a member of the Working Committee of the Students' Federation (Socialist Group), arrested with objectionable papers!'

A third paper wrote: 'Famous Bengali member of the Socialist Front, Mr Rai, made state guest.'

If one were asked to tell the truth, Class I political prisoners get far better treatment in the jail than they would in their own homes. Food, drink, reading and writing material—there is no shortage of anything. My days passed in perfect contentment. Miss Rossa was released on the second day itself, but the court sentenced me to three years' imprisonment. I thought I would be rid of the party's ghost once and for all, but the Quit India movement was launched in 1942. The jail was filled to overflowing. In no time at all, the party disease spread like an epidemic all through the jail. Free food, long hours of sleep, endless arguments at the top of one's voice—that is all we did all day long. The Communist population was virtually negligible in our jail. They were so few that they made no attempt to make their presence felt. The devotees of Gandhi *baba* considered public discourse and argument as much part of their party's mandate as spinning the *charkha*. They preferred to stay away from controversies and regarded even raising their voice in protest against the bad behaviour of the jail authorities as a form of violence. The Socialists were in a majority and I considered it expedient to declare myself as one of them. A few days later I learnt that the Communist Party was working hard to have its members released from prison. Everything I saw and heard convinced me that soon they would have all their members freed. So one day I stole the chance to tell the Communists to remember to include me among their numbers. And while I knew no discomfort in jail, I yearned, day and night, to be free.

Escape from jail meant freedom from the quagmire of the party. And the more I struggled to escape from this quicksand, the more I got sucked in. I would read books on existentialism by day to erase the Kingdom of God from my mind and at night, in bed, weep bitterly for hours and pray to God for my release. Finally, God heard my entreaties and I fell ill. My illness began to have the desired effect. Newspapers began to demand my freedom. Finally, the government's attention was drawn and I was shifted to the General Hospital for proper medical care. My treatment began and I started gaining weight. The fever began to go down, but the biggest fallout was that I was free of the ghosts of the party. Well-educated, pretty nurses, sent on ARP training, looked after me. I found they were all oddly reserved with me. One day, when I tried to find out the reason for their curtness, the *chakra* of the party—the *chakra* I had read about in the Panchtantra tales—began to dance around my head. They were keeping their distance because they thought I was an acolyte of Gandhi. And the followers of Gandhi, they believed, had betrayed Subhash Bose. Inspired by an unknown impulse, I criticised the Gandhians and they began to inundate me with a hundred questions—aimed towards making the discovery that I was a Forward Blocist. From now on, it was as though they could not stay a single minute without me. It was good that the government showed every sign of intelligence and released me, or else I would have been the victim of a new disease.

Upon my release, I vowed that I would run for my life whenever anyone so much as mentioned a party. I tried my best but I did bump into one member of a party, sooner rather than later. He was an old acquaintance and so it was difficult to avoid him. We got talking and he eventually opened up the Pandora's Box of his party. Handing me the Declaration favouring the 'Ray Project' as opposed to the 'Bombay Project', he said, 'Look here, this is the project propounded by Comrade Ray.' Any arguments would have only pulled me into further debate, and the pro-Ray gentleman would never have left me either had I not ventured to give an opinion. So, the moment I said, 'It is good,' he relented.

By the time I reached home, the newspapers had already announced: 'Soon after his release, in a statement Comrade Prafull branded the Bombay Project as exploitative. It can in no way be compared with the Ray Project. The Ray Project, he said, is in every sense the project that will bring relief to the downtrodden.'

My studies had come to a standstill. My family began to clamour for my marriage. Till my sojourn in jail, I was considered hot property in the marriage market, and there was a queue of people wanting to marry their girls to me. But now most people with marriageable daughters believed that giving their daughter in marriage to a no-good wastrel like me was like pushing her into a well. Still, this did not stop the stubborn father of one fortunate girl from believing in my prospects. I gave in to my parents' entreaties. A meeting was set up with the bride's family. I reached their home in my best plumes. I was given the best possible reception befitting a future son-in-law. The girl's father was a man of modern views and held many opinions on the world and its affairs. Soon after the business of 'seeing' the girl was done, he launched into a tirade on global politics. He talked. I listened. After sometime, I sensed that the crowd on the other side of the curtain was anxious to hear my views. I feared they might decide to take me for a yes-man and eliminate me. One look at my prospective wife and I had already begun to construct several modern bungalows in the new style.

Perforce, I now had to step into the battleground. Talk had now veered towards the Quit India movement. My prospective father-in-law maintained that the Congress had committed a childish mistake in passing the Quit India resolution. I could not let this go unchallenged. The atmosphere became charged. I also sensed the hat on the other side of the curtain. My voice rose four-fold and I went so far as to say, 'Our goal is not far now. Since 1942 the country is…'

'Listen!' my one and only prospective brother-in-law stepped out of his room and stopped me mid-sentence. With complete trust in his youth, I said, 'Yes, Mohan Babu, tell me if I am wrong?'

He sat down and began to speak in a grave tone, 'Well, look here, Prafull Babu, I have been quietly listening to you all this while. For as long as I could, I suppressed my soul and controlled myself. But now that things have reached such a pass, to stay quiet is tantamount to being unfaithful to one's salt.'

'Certainly, certainly! Of course!' I said enthusiastically.

'Your last few pronouncements are things that can only be said by Socialists and fall within the purview of the Defence of India Rules. As far as I can tell, surely you appreciate the importance of doing one's duty. In the present situation I am failing to do my duty, and what is it, then, if not being unfaithful to my salt, tell me…' he pulled out a cigarette from his father's cigarette case and began to puff at it.

His father looked at me, smiled and said, 'Well, this is the first time I have seen my son so serious.'

'What are you saying?' asked a voice from behind the curtain. 'The boy is in a new job. And look at you, instead of trying to get him a promotion, you are about to fix up with a bomb-maker so that our boy loses his job! Let my daughter stay unmarried; we don't need to have anything to do with such types.'

This angry voice probably belonged to my mother-in-law. I couldn't understand what was going on till someone explained to me that Mohan Babu had been working with the Secret Services since

1943. And this was the first time in his entire period of service that he was letting an offender against the Defence of India Rules go, despite seeing him with his own eyes and listening to his perfidious talk with his own ears. He did, however, show me sufficient leniency, giving me two hours to make good my escape.

I took barely fifteen minutes to get ready and not just 'quit' their house but also 'quit' whatever was left of my hopes of getting married. The lucky girl stood by the window and struck a sorrowful pose as she gazed out. I could clearly see the tears in her large eyes, but besides drawing a deep breath, what else could I do?

I took up a job in a small commercial district, thinking it would be far removed from party politics. But I have soon found out the reality—there are thousands of parties here. It is impossible to walk even a few steps by distancing oneself from one or the other party. If you laugh and joke with Mr A, Mr B takes offence. If I go take tuitions in the home of Pandit C, Munshi D gets into a huff. Mr E is a mill owner. One day I accepted an invitation to his house and had barely eaten a spoonful of *kheer* that I found I had brought shame to the entire *Capital* by Karl Marx. Forget about the big shops, even the pavement vendors have their own party. One day I discovered that cigarettes had disappeared from the market. You could find smokers searching for cigarettes even in hardware and utility shops. I asked Shri Shivaji, the man who got me my tea and cigarettes from where he managed to procure his cigarettes. He grinned and said, 'Sir, for our party-*wallahs*... what to do... we get it from the black market.' It didn't take me long to figure out that I was smoking my cigarettes thanks to the party and that I belonged to his party.

Ever since the Congress declared its intention to enter the electoral fray, I can see my friends change colours. All those who had sworn before the *sarkar bahadur*[5] that they would have nothing to do with

[5] Referring to the colonial government.

any party, have taken out the Gandhi caps they had had laundered and tucked away in their boxes after 1942[6]. And those who used to look around in both directions before even uttering the word 'Congress', now stop people on the streets and wax eloquent about it. I too can now declare myself as belonging to a party. I have little interest left in the Communists because Miss Rossa has married an American soldier and brought her international principles to real practice. Everyone is bent on lavishing liberal praise upon the Socialists and there is very little difference left between the Forward Bloc and the Congress. The path is clear. But the moment someone raises the subject of a party, my heartbeats slow down and my head begins to spin. No matter how hard I try, how can I stay still? All day long, the questions fly thick and fast:

'Mr D and Mr E are both thinking of standing on the Congress ticket. Who, in your opinion, is better suited?'

'Hadn't the government filed a suit against Mr M?'

'Have you heard, Raja Sahib will be standing against the Congress?'

'Arre, Sahib, Mr T is standing on the Hindu Sabha[7] plank. He is your dear friend; you will have to help him.'

And so it goes on.

At such times, I become utterly quiet. My silence is being so interpreted that every party*wallah* now thinks that I know all the secrets of their opponent's party. This compounds the confusion. I belong to all parties; I belong to no party. One can't live without identifying with any party, and yet whenever the question, 'Which party?' is put to me, my head begins to spin.

I get neither peace during day nor sleep at night. And, if perchance I do sleep, I am plagued by nightmares. I see that I am running on a road. A ragtag bunch of urchins follow me, beating a

[6] The year refers to the Quit India movement.

[7] Right-wing Hindu organisation.

tin drum and shouting, 'Which party? Which party?' Exasperated, I run to beat them, but they pelt me with stones and clap their hands as they keep teasing me. Once again I start running on the road. A tailor calls out, 'This road belongs to Party A!' I get off the main road and dive into a side street. A barber calls out, 'This street belongs to Party B!' I hurry out of the side street and fall into a drain… I wake up and find I have fallen out of my bed. I don't have the strength to get up. Buddhan, who looks after me and is suffering from black fever, somehow manages to get me off the floor and back into my bed. He consoles me by saying, 'This is nothing.' One day he will go to his village and fetch his uncle, who will exorcise me of my devils and make me all right. I am haunted by a ghost, he tells me, an evil spirit.

I agree with him. I am indeed bedeviled by a ghost. I beseech all those who dismiss ghosts and apparitions as superstitious nonsense, to believe, at least, in this ghost.

Splendour

That I would see Fatima Di[1] again, and see her in such a state, I had never imagined. And so I stood, lost in a trance, in the shoe shop in the middle of the Patna Market as though I was in paradise. In front of me stood two women, clad from head to toe in burqa and with them was a nine- or ten-year-old girl, pretty as a doll. The girl repeated her question to me, 'Aunty asks when did you return to Patna?'

The shopkeeper addressed me as he counted his change, 'She is asking you.'

The girl laughed. Laughter also tinkled from inside the burqa. It was a familiar laugh. The girl laughed again, this time at something said to her by her aunt. She said, 'My aunty is your Fatima Di.'

Now I could clearly hear Fatima Di's ever-so-familiar voice from behind the brown burqa, 'I heard that you live in Delhi or Bombay?'

'I have been in Patna for the past ten years.'

'How strange! Here you are in Patna and I have not seen you!'

[1] Di is short for Didi, and is used a little more informally to convey an affectionate regard for an older woman who is considered like an elder sister.

'And you?' I asked as I slowly regained my senses.

The burqa-clad Fatima Di cut me short and said, 'Forget about me...Tell me about yourself. Did you marry?'

She saw me getting flustered and quickly said, 'Have you seen Danish Manzil in Baqarganj Gali? I live there. Will you come there one day with your wife? Why don't you come tomorrow, at eight in the morning?'

The girl piped up, 'We have to go to Hamida aunty's house tomorrow at eight,'

'Oh-oh...Well, then, the day after?'

Instinctively, the word, *Pranam,* escaped my lips as I took my leave.

She said, 'Stay well.'

We never greeted Fatima Di by the customary *Adaab Arz.*[3] She would always accept our *Pranam* and in return bless us with her 'Stay well'. But we had never seen Fatima Di covered from head to toe in a burqa before. Not even in the days when she had gone into hiding from prying eyes.

I couldn't sleep that night. A shadow, dressed in a brown burqa, would appear before me the moment I closed my eyes... a pair of latticed eyes danced before me. No matter how hard I tried, I couldn't remove the burqa to look at Fatima Di's face. In frustration, I would open my eyes.

A lesser woman would become suspicious if her husband tossed and turned all night and drew long, deep sighs. But a writer's wife knows well enough that a writer becomes restless and sleepless when he is in the throes of writing a story. And so, she sleeps on peacefully.

But that night she happened to be awake. I asked her, 'Have I ever told you about Fatima Di?'

[2] A Hindu greeting.

[3] A Muslim greeting, less formal than the traditional *Assalam Aleikum* (or the abbreviated *Salaam*).

'No, never. Who is Fatima Di?'

'The Fatima Di of one of my stories,' I said, not wishing to give her any more details, and turned away.

The Fatima Di of stories! I was surprised that I had never told my wife about Fatima Di. Actually, come to think of it, there was no reason for surprise. Knowing she was the daughter of a Sanatani[4] and the sister of a hardcore Hindu Mahasabha-ite, I had deliberately never told her about Fatima Di. I was afraid she would make a face and say something. Or, she might just dismiss it as 'Absurd!'

No, not absurd. She was extraordinary!

Even thirty-six years ago people had said, 'Abnormal…Half-mad!'

It was my good fortune that I had had the opportunity to see this extraordinary woman at close quarters.

I remembered that assembly in 1930. A massive crowd had gathered in the school backyard. Many people wearing Gandhi caps were seated on the platform. A ten- or eleven-year-old girl stood delivering a lecture. I had been surprised to see a girl wearing a kurta and pajama. Someone said she was the daughter of the Maulvi from Sonpur. Maulvi Sahab had taken to wearing coarse *khadi* cloth and spinning the *charkha* from the days of the Khilafat[5]. And his daughter stood in front of the crowd dressed in a white kurta-pajama, carrying the tricolour on her shoulder.

I saw her for the second time shortly after the devastating earthquake of 1934. She seemed to have grown up quite a bit in

[4] Follower of Sanatan Dharam, one who accepts the traditional, immemorial, centuries-old understanding of Hinduism; generally used for those who ascribe to the more orthodox Hindu beliefs.

[5] The call for the Khilafat movement was given by the Ali brothers, Maulana Mohamed and Shaukat Ali, and supported by Gandhiji around 1920, expressing the solidarity and support of the Indian Muslims to the Turkish Caliphate.

the last four years. Mahatma Gandhi had come on a tour of the earthquake-affected areas. I had not had the slightest difficulty in recognising the girl who stood on the dais next to Gandhiji. There she was, Maulvi Sahab's daughter, reciting verses from the Holy Quran in her clear voice at the all-faiths prayer meeting. I was told she had just come out of prison, after spending two years behind bars. People said she had been brutally beaten and wounded by the stick-wielding policemen at the time of her arrest.

And then again, in 1937, I got the first opportunity to see her up close. The district's political parties had organised a function in the school compound. Those were the days when the Congress held sway. Therefore the delegates were staying on the school premises and the students had joined the Congress Party volunteers in looking after the various arrangements. That was the time when I had first addressed Maulvi Sahab's daughter, the General Officer Commanding of the Sevadal, as 'Fatima Di'. The Muslim League workers had tried to disrupt the proceedings during Professor Azeemabadi's speech. Fatima Di had leapt onto the stage and her strong voice had echoed in the marquee, 'Traitors! You should be ashamed of yourselves!'

And then, in 1943, I had to stay with her almost day and night for five months. Resplendent images of the firebrand Fatima Di walking about the lanes and alleys of Banaras, Lucknow, Allahabad and Gorakhpur, with her band of Azaad Dasta[6] spreading the spark of revolution, dance before my eyes. How she had answered each one of the coarse obscenities that the police sergeant had showered upon her at the time of arresting her, and the anger that had slashed across her face like lightning! And the glow on her face when she had faced rampaging mobs during the communal riots of 1947! How did the brown burqa cover all that? How did this happen?

I wanted to rip the curtain that had fallen across her face, rip it into tiny pieces. I wanted to see Fatima Di's face but she covered her

[6] Meaning the 'Free Platoon'.

face with both her palms, screaming, 'No, no! Aju!...Ajit!...Don't look at my face!'

I snapped out of my dream and lay still for a long time. The 'signature tune' of the All India Radio heralded a new dawn. Suddenly a thought arose in my mind: 'How come no one had begun an agitation to change the signature tune of Akashvani[7]? It is almost entirely lifted from the pure sound of the *Azaan*...the rising and falling sound of the muezzin transposed on the strings of the violin.'

*

As I climbed the stairs of Danish Manzil, I felt as though every brick of this venerable old building was looking at me with astonishment.

'Whom do you want to meet?'

'Fatima Di.'

'Who?'

'Fatima Di.'

The person asking this question stood transfixed before me, like a statue. Then he whispered in bewilderment, 'Fatima Di?'

Suddenly the pretty, doll-like girl appeared, laughing and saying *Salaam* to me. She asked, 'Aunty asks why you haven't brought your wife with you?'

I understood; Fatima Di would not appear before me even today. She would conduct the conversation through the girl.

I could hear several doors slam loudly around me. The radios that had been playing at medium volume were suddenly switched off. The air became sibilant with hushed, whispered conversations.

'So, you weave tales, do you?' The question was posed from behind a curtain.

I gazed at the tattered *durrie* spread on the floor and answered, 'Yes, I have made a profession of my habit of lying...'

[7] Popular government-owned radio service.

Several windows inside Danish Manzil creaked open at the sound of her tinkling laughter. The room became heavy with the smell of frying onions and it reminded me of a recent incident in which a young man had been arrested with a bottle of 'killer poison' in the kitchen of the NCC camp. What had been the young Muslim's name?

The doll-like girl was called Naghma. She brought a cup of tea for me. I wanted to refuse but couldn't. 1 took the cup in my hand and asked, 'So, Fatima Di, for all these days…I mean…where did you disappear?'

She answered 'When will you come with your wife?'

I closed my eyes and drank the tea in one gulp. I understood: Fatima Di did not wish to answer my question. In fact, I now began to harbour a serious doubt. Surely, this lady could not be my Fatima Di, she was someone else.

I got up from the chair. Naghma brought a *paan* on a plate. This time I resorted to a white lie. I said, 'I don't eat *paan*.'

As I turned to go, I found the courage to say, 'Excuse me, but I believe that you are not my Fatima Di...'

'You are right, Aziz.'

Aziz? I was startled. Fatima Di used to call me Aziz[8] instead of Ajit. I stood silently. A tinkling laugh broke out on the other side of the curtain.

As I came down the stairs of Danish Manzil, I felt as though every brick of that venerable old building was looking at me with loathing. I tried hard to recall the name of the young man who had poisoned the food of a thousand NCC cadets.

I saw an Urdu poster being pasted on a wall in front of the Amjadiya Hotel. It proclaimed in bold letters, 'Down with the Nationalist Muslim Convention!…Beware of Traitors!'

[8] Aziz, a popular Muslim name, means close friend, relative or dear one.

Seeing that hate-filled poster, a Maulana began to mumble, 'These wretches have taken to whipping the passions of the community instead of sticking to their old profession of carding cotton. They will have to be taught a lesson, these sons of nationalists!'

I began to feel nauseous. I hailed a rickshaw, sat down and felt my pulse. My heart was racing. My body was drenched in sweat...The tea had a bitter after-taste, didn't it? The General Hospital was on my right; the police station on my left. I wondered where I should go first.

But when the rickshaw puller asked me my destination, I said, 'Take me to Rajendra Nagar.'

*

Having sat through a four-hour long symposium on 'The New Story, The Non Story, The Story of Today, and The Story of Tomorrow', without uttering a word in the discussion that followed, I didn't have the strength to go back home. In such situations, one has to recover one's poise either on the banks of the Ganga or in a bar. But when the rickshaw puller asked me my destination, I said, 'Take me to Rajendra Nagar.'

By the time I reached Gole Market. I could, as always, see my flat from a distance. I saw a light in my room and became apprehensive. Where would I go now?

I resolved to excuse myself to whoever it was. I would make an excuse and bid them an early farewell.

As I climbed the stairs, I carried the burden of all the woes and worries of the world. I knocked on the door, wearing the mask of a man deeply disgruntled with the world at large. But when the door opened, I saw my wife, her face wreathed in smiles. She looked so happy that she did not even notice my woebegone expression. She chirped as soon as I stepped in, 'Guess who is here?'

I did not even get the chance to be surprised. A smiling Naghma appeared before me and did a *Salaam.* My wife exclaimed, 'Oh-ho, we have been laughing for the past three hours…Where have you been? And you are a strange one! You never told me!'

'Told you what?' I asked.

'That you are a Musalman, and not a Hindu,' said a voice from my room.

I looked and found Fatima Di sitting there in all her splendid glory. Her burqa lay on the floor—torn to shreds.

'How did this happen? Who...?'

My wife said, 'Who else? Your darling daughter, Nomi…she kept barking till the burqa was taken off. And when the burqa was taken off, she ripped it apart with her teeth.'

'Where is she?'

I saw the naughty wretch lying cuddled in Fatima Di's lap, hiding. She always does that…She makes a face and sits huddled just like that whenever she does something wrong.

'She refuses to get off her lap and growls when we tell her to,' said Naghma.

I was seeing Fatima Di after nineteen or twenty years; she hadn't changed a bit. There were some new lines around her eyes; that was all.

My wife broke into laughter every few minutes. She launched into her high-spirited narration. 'I tied Nomi up and opened the door. She asked me, "Is Aziz at home?"…I said, "Aziz? No, there is no Aziz, there is Ajit." Then she said. "Yes, yes, I heard that he has altered a few letters in his name and become a Hindu, and has married some poor Hindu girl." I was stunned...'

'See, Bhabhijaan is still under some illusion. What do you say, Aziz? You have despoiled her religion. Tell me, what is this if not *kufr*? But I tell you, hats off to you! You are one sharp player! After turning into an idol worshipper, you chose a bearded god for yourself who recited the *kalima* and...'

We saw her gesticulating in the direction of the portrait of Shri Ramakrishna Paramahansa[9] and burst out laughing.

[9] The mystic saint who was the spiritual master of Swami Vivekananda. He was born on 18 February 1836 in Kamarpukur in Hooghly district of West Bengal.

When the waves of laughter subsided, 1 asked. 'So, tell me. where have you been? Where *are* you?'

'I *was* in the grave; I *am* in the grave.'

My wife went into the kitchen. I felt I had asked the question at an inappropriate time. Fatima Di asked, 'What did you think?...That I had gone to Pakistan? Didn't you?'

'Why did you leave politics?'

'Why do you ask me that? Why don't you ask those sons of the elites and the Nawabs, who turned overnight into patriots and entered the Congress camp, hiding their daggers in their sleeves? Why don't you seek the answer from your leaders? Why don't you ask them why those Muslim League-ists who went about burning the national flag and abusing Gandhi-Jawahar-Patel, were showered with praises while those who shed their sweat and blood for the nation were removed from the scene like flies from milk?...Why don't you ask yourself these questions?' Fatima Di's face went red. I was pleased.

Yet I interrupted her tirade, 'But why did you remain quiet?'

'Quiet?' The word erupted like the roar of an angry lioness. 'What would you know of the cruelties they showered on me?...And the doors I knocked on—what would you know of those? But every good soul—from Patna to Delhi—merely advised me to take their sage counsel and get married, raise children. And when all else failed—there were the threats...Oh!...Aziz!'

Fatima Di was close to tears. I didn't know when my wife had come to stand beside me. She rebuked me, 'You are a strange man!'

Nomi, who had been quiet all this while, now began to sniff Fatima Di's face and make soft mewling sounds.

'People have still not come to their senses. They still run after positions. The country can go to hell for all they care!' An intense pain had crept into Fatima Di's voice. 'You write stories, don't you? Do you remember all the talk of Hindu-Muslim unity in the poems and stories of the progressive writers; the pleas of humankind above all else and god knows what else. And immediately after independence, not only did they stop talking, but also started singing a different tune. All those who had once pledged their lives to the nation and its people, stood mute as the python of communalism gobbled up the entire nation.'

My wife interrupted by saying, 'Fatima Di, the food will get cold.'

Preparations are underway at the Town Hall to celebrate the Nationalist Muslim Conference with lot of fanfare. The newspapers are full of reports of delegates arriving from different parts of the country. And in the same newspapers, there are reports of opposition to this very conference. Every day, accounts are being published from both sides, each accompanied with hundreds of names, both for and against. The opposition claims that there are no 'non-nationalists'; all Muslims are nationalists. Whereas those who proclaim themselves to be nationalists go about saying openly that the old Muslim Leaguers are nothing but dyed-in-the-wool communalists, poisoned to the core by the venom of communal politics, and that they should never be trusted.

I hadn't attended a political function for a long time. This time I went, thinking it was my duty to do so. But once I saw the sight that prevailed at the venue, I stopped stock-still by the roadside.

Thousands of people stood shouting slogans on either side of the road in front of the Town Hall. Gunfire, slogans, showers of stones and bricks, rent the air.

The policemen stood quietly in a row because the sons of several 'low-caste' Muslim leaders and sundry high officials were patronising the protestors. I felt as though we had gone back to the year 1947. That same frenzy in the air, the same faces, the same scenes.

'Catch him! Catch him! There goes that son of an infidel!'

'Tadd-taddak! Tadd-taddak!'

'Here's the bastard! Beat the swine!'

'Son of a pig!'

'Tadd-taddak!'

Now they began to catch hold of every delegate and proceed to beat them up. The frenzy reached a crescendo. Slogans, gunshots, pellets and stones, began to rain down like hailstones.

'Long live Mahatama Gandhi!'

A thin but strong voice rang out. Suddenly everything stopped. Everyone turned in the direction of the voice. At the entrance of the Anjuman Islamiya Hall—the Abdul Bari Gate—stood a woman raising slogans.

Fatima Di? Was it her? I could not believe my eyes.

'Who is that woman?'

'Must be some Hindu.'

'Oh no…Don't you recognise her? It is that same bitch...'

'Fatima?…*Saali,* she has shown up again?'

'Bitch!'

A group of mad men charged towards Fatima Di, dancing and showering the choicest obscenities. Fatima Di kept standing there, smiling at the mob. Within a matter of minutes the barbarians had flung her to the ground. Then they began to drag her by her hair. The crowd on either side of the road egged them on, clapping their hands and shouting, 'Well done!' By the time the clutch of policemen reached the spot, the mob had ripped off Fatima Di's clothes…Beyond that, I could see no more.

After several days, we gathered our courage and went to see Fatima Di in the hospital.

We met Naghma at the door of her cabin. She saw us and broke into loud sobs.

'The animals poured a bottle of acid on Fatima Di's face. Her face is completely charred. One eye is gone. One hand is broken.

Fatima Di's lips quivered as she heard us approach. Perhaps she was trying to smile. Then she said in a low voice, 'Go away, you silly boy! Have you come here to cry? See, see the splendour! *Bhabhi*…make that thing and bring it tomorrow…*Paayas*…no, what is it called?…*Parmaan.* And bring Nomi along.'

That I would see Fatima Di like this, I had never imagined.

Glossary

Agahan: the ninth month of the Hindu lunar year, corresponding to November-December

Arre: an often-used exclamation to convey a variety of reactions ranging from surprise, pleasure, dismay, horror; sometimes also used as prefix to another word, such as Arre Bhai, a form of address or proclamation

Ashtami: the eighth day of a lunar fortnight

Ashwin: the first lunar mansion (in Aries)

Azaan: the muezzin's call to Muslims to come for prayer, given five times a day

Babu: a prefix to denote respect

Babua: an affectionate form of address for a younger male

Bahu/Bahuriya: daughter-in-law

Baisakh: the second of the twelve lunar months of the Hindu calendar, corresponding to April-May

Bangalin: a Bengali woman

Bappa: father

Beedi: hand-rolled tobacco leaf containing a pinch of tobacco

Bhauji: respectful form of address for elder brother's wife

Bhaiya: brother

Bhabhi: sister-in-law

Bhooja: parched or roasted grain or rice

Bigha: a measure of land (the official or *sarkari bigha* equals about one-fifth of an acre; the *kutcha* or unofficial *bigha* varies from a quarter to a third of an acre)

Bindi: a dot of vermillion worn on the forehead, usually by married women. Fancier versions can have bits of tinsel or glitter stuck to it, such as the one worn by Jhumki, to add to the sparkle

Bitiya: an affectionate form of address for a younger female, who is being addressed as a daughter

Boondi: tiny sweets, like drops

Burqa: all-encompassing outer garment worn, usually, by Muslim women

Chait: the first month of the Hindu lunar year, corresponding to March-April; the crop harvested during this month is the spring harvest

Chappal: open-toed footwear

Charkha: the wheel used for spinning

Chhee: an exclamation to convey disgust, shame, horror, rebuke

Chik: a hanging screen or blind made of finely split bamboo or reeds, placed horizontally and strung together in often elaborate patterns with twine

Chooda/chewra: rice boiled, pounded and roasted; dunked in curd it is called *dahi chewra*

Chowk: main square or crossroad in a marketplace or busy part of a city or town

CID: Crime Investigation Department, a department of secret police that investigates heinous crimes, often those with inter-state ramifications

Dhoti: a length of fabric tied around the waist to cover the lower part of the body

Durrie: coarse cotton rug

Gamcha: a cloth or towel, usually worn slung over one shoulder; this is a multi-purpose accessory unique to rural India; it serves to protect from the elements, wipe one's face and neck of sweat, rain, etc, and can be bundled under the head a bit like a pillow while traveling

Ganja: leaves, flower heads or buds of the hemp plant *(Cannabis sativa)*

Garam masala: assorted spices such as pepper corns, cinnamon, cardamom, cumin, cloves, nutmeg, etc, roasted and ground together; used as a popular garnish or added to food while cooking

Gur: raw sugar, made from boiling sugarcane juice

Haarsinghar: the tree *Nyctanthes arbor tristis*; has fragrant tiny white and orange flowers

Haat: market, in remote areas it could be a weekly open-air market; there are also specialised *haat*s, such as those, for example, dealing only with cattle

Halwa: a sweet concoction made of ghee, sugar and flour among other condiments

Haveli: a large, grand house or mansion

Hukkah: a pipe for smoking tobacco through water

Huzoor: a form of address to one in a position of authority, or of a higher rank

Jajim: a cotton sheet, with a checkered or figurative pattern, spread on the floor or over a carpet or rug

Jalebi: a sweet made of flour, shaped like a doodle, soaked in syrup

Janeo: the sacred thread worn from adolescence onwards by males of the upper three caste groups

Janta: the people

Ji: a deferential suffix

Kadhi: a dish made from gram flour, turmeric, sour curds and spices, often with fried dumplings made of gram flour floating in it

Kaka: a deferential form of address for an older man, maybe unrelated, or an older cousin, uncle, or neighbour

Kalima: the Muslim profession of faith—*La illaha il Allah Muhammad ur Rasool Allah*—There is no God but God and Muhammad is His Prophet

Kartik: the eighth month of the Hindu lunar year, corresponding to October-November

Kasbah: a small town or a large village, it was an integral unit of pre-partition India, and evocative of a distinct cultural, social, historical, linguistic identity

Khadi: hand-spun coarse cotton fabric, such as that spun by Gandhi and made popular by him

Koka: nail, spike, thorn

Kos: a measure of distance, approximately equal to two miles

Kshatriya: a member of the second *varna* or caste group of ancient Indo-Aryan society; its members were warriors

Kufr: unbelief or impiety according to the Muslim faith

Kulfi: a frozen sweet

Laddoo: round balls of sweetened flour mixed with ghee

Ma/Maiya: mother

Mahavirji: a title for the god Hanuman

Mang tikka: an ornament worn by women in the parting of the hair, its tip dangles on the forehead

Maulvi: a Muslim learned man, one versed in the Holy Quran

Mem: a title for a westernised or anglicised woman

Mohulla: neighborhood, locality

Moong dal: a type of lentil with small, yellow, oval grains

Mothi: a kind of grass

Murgh mussallam: an entire chicken, marinated and cooked in a clay oven in the Mughlai style of cooking

Nirguna bhakti: a form of worship where the deity, one without attributes, is worshipped—a form of devotion to the unqualified, ultimate being

Paan: betel leaf, usually eaten with a bit of lime and catechu paste and several other (optional) spices and nuts

Panchayat: a council of five (in olden times only men, now women too are included); it served as judge, jury, arbiter and umpire for all village matters, both individual/personal and social

Pandit/panditji: a Hindu learned man, could also refer to the temple priest

Phua: paternal aunt

Pucca: permanent or lasting, used for roads, houses and other forms of construction
Puja: worship or adoration of a deity through rituals
Puri: a type of bread, round, puffed up and deep-fried
Rasgulla: round balls of dough, deep-fried and soaked in syrup
Sattu: coarse flour made from parched grain; the flour can be eaten on its own as a snack or mixed with water and a little *gur* as a nourishing drink; it can also be carried tied in a cloth bundle on a journey, as it keeps well in all seasons and is an instant and inexpensive form of nourishment
Saali: literally, wife's sister; however, it is used as coarse exclamation, a popular term of abuse for a female
Sahab/Sahib: an honorific added to a name to denote respect
Sanjivani: a life-restoring herb said to have been carried by Hanuman to save the life of Lakshman during the battle against the forces of Ravana
Supari: areca nut, also called betel nut, chewed on its own or with betel leaves and tobacco
Taka: a copper coin worth two former *pice;* it is no longer in use
Thali: a large dish usually made of copper, used to serve and eat from
Thana: police station
Tola/Toli: quarter of a village or town
Tonga: horse-drawn carriage
Vaid: Ayurvedic physician
Viraha: a state of separation from the beloved